Death at Ten Paces

Thornton was waiting for him, the Russian springblade held tightly in both hands, his body prone in the middle of the floor.

The assassin swung his beastlike frame into the doorway, swinging the riot gun in a wide arc in front of him. Bo allowed his aiming instinct to go on automatic pilot. Depressing the firing lever, Bo felt the razor-edge blade fly free from the handle, a slight rasping sound escaping from the weapon as the spring released its several hundred pounds of pent-up energy.

The forged missile impaled the target's heart within a single massive beat . . .

MACHETE
by Greg Walker

Books in the SPRINGBLADE series
by Greg Walker

SPRINGBLADE
MACHETE

STILETTO
(coming in April)

MACHETE
GREG WALKER

CHARTER BOOKS, NEW YORK

MACHETE

A Charter Book/published by arrangement with
the author

PRINTING HISTORY
Charter edition/January 1990

ISBN: 1-55773-294-9

Charter Books are published by The Berkley Publishing Group,
200 Madison Avenue, New York, New York 10016
The name "Charter" and the "C" logo are trademarks belonging
to Charter Communications Inc.

PRINTED IN THE UNITED STATES OF AMERICA

10 9 8 7 6 5 4 3 2 1

For Tom, 5th Special Forces Group (Airborne), Republic of Vietnam. Though you're in a sanctuary not of your own choosing, just remember to keep your feet and knees together, bro. They can kill us, but they can't eat us.

ACKNOWLEDGMENTS

Great credit goes to Al Mar, whose knowledge base of combat cutlery is my greatest resource when arming Thornton and his team with their lethal hardware. Also, I must thank my agent, Ethan Ellenberg. His support and insightful suggestions are always welcome guests in my home. Finally, my sincere hope that all those forced to flee from their homelands because of political tyranny will one day find themselves living as free men and women in houses they build on land that they own.

Freedom, contrary to popular thought, is not free.

G.A.W.
12 January, 1989

CHAPTER 1

■■■■■■■■

SANCTUARY!

The hot muggy scent of the day's slaughter wafted toward Melendez, its thick aroma encouraging his nostrils to expand and contract with pleasure. It had been a profitable morning, he thought to himself. In under three hours his men had, by various means, killed exactly seventy-three *subersivos*; expertly stacking their corpses alongside the hand-dug pits that would be their graves by day's end.

Melendez was pleased. Before him, neatly arranged and in impeccable order, were his notes. A man who prided himself on recognizing opportunity no matter what its form, he had begun evaluating the many weapons systems being offered to his government by using them on days like today. As a respected member of the army's Ordnance Evaluation Team, Melendez was considered an expert in light infantry weapons and their effects on the human condition. Arms merchants sought him out during their visits to the capital, knowing that a favorable report from his ancient field desk would make their efforts worthwhile.

Already he had decided to recommend the purchase of fifty of South Africa's newest light machine gun. His men were highly impressed with the weapon, and the two made available to them had made short work of the huddled masses he had assigned as targets. He possessed a great respect for the South African arms industry; never a bad product from those "chicos" yet.

A more valuable piece of equipment, at least in his mind, was the sleek German submachine gun which rested within arm's reach. Unlike earlier models, the H&K SMG II featured a removable suppressor and high-velocity/low-velocity switch lever, allowing the use of standard 9mm ammunition at supersonic or subsonic speeds. This was, in the major's mind, a very economical approach to the high cost of bullets these days. Leave it to the Germans, Melendez reminded himself as he emptied a silent torrent of copper-jacketed hornets into a living test dummy. They hadn't lost their touch in these matters despite losing two world wars.

He would request twenty-five of this item for his unit alone.

The blast of three rapid detonations told him that Corporal Rios had successfully exploded the American claymore mines into a third batch of hapless "volunteers." Knowing each mine contained roughly seven hundred individual .30 caliber steel balls, and that these were propelled by the awesome force of a full pound of C-4 explosive going off behind them, the major held no doubt as to what the combined effect of three mines had been. Although leery of selling the devices to the dictatorship of Colonel Arturo Aguilar, the United States did agree to provide a limited amount of claymores on an introductory basis. Melendez chuckled to himself at the thought, knowing even before the Polaroid pictures were handed to him by a breathless runner that the "introduction" had been successful.

Using a hand-held magnifying glass, he carefully inspected the series of color photos. Satisfied, he dismissed the young soldier and scribbled several comments concerning the results in his note pad. Clipping the ghastly pictures into an album he kept for his own entertainment, Melendez was reminded by the hamburgerlike appearance of his victims that it was nearly time for lunch.

Upon issuing the order for an hour's break, Major Luis Melendez stood and stretched his camouflaged frame, then carefully adjusted the custom-tailored shoulder holster which housed the big Sig-Sauer .45 automatic he carried at all times. Casually rubbing the small of his powerful back with both hands, he assured himself that the Gerber Mk I boot knife he'd purchased while attending jump school at Fort Benning was within easy reach. Melendez was a careful man, knowing after six long years of guerrilla warfare that it was the careful who kept breathing, while others died foolishly.

Luis Adolfo Garcia Melendez was a career man. Born in a

shithole that passed itself off as one of La Libertad's larger coastal towns, Luis learned at an early age that life in his country held less value than the gaudy trinkets bought by the gringos that visited year round. At sixteen he killed a boyhood friend in an argument over a wallet they'd found. Never apprehended, Melendez discovered that not only did crime pay, but that certain crimes paid better than others. Recognizing his ability to murder without remorse, Luis began to hire himself out as a contract killer. It hadn't taken long for his reputation to reach the ears of a certain captain in military intelligence, who ordered the young man brought before him in chains. Offered a choice between prison or service to his country, Melendez chose a patriot's calling and began honing his talents as a member of the captain's special-assignments unit.

Now, at age thirty-five, Melendez commanded his own unit of specialists. The captain who had recognized his unique talents had become a colonel, then president of La Libertad in a bloody coup which, in turn, gave birth to the guerrilla insurgency that had now been waging for six long years. Supported by the United States because of Colonel Arturo Aguilar's rabid anticommunist stance in Central America, the dictatorship witnessed the fall of Somoza's Nicaragua, vowing that the same would not happen to it. To accomplish this goal, Aguilar decreed that his forces would use any means possible to fight the guerrillas, regardless of the cost.

Now, as he casually approached the mobile kitchen which was feeding the noon meal, Melendez reminded himself of the mission entrusted him by Aguilar at last night's meeting. As he considered its importance, the major was unaware of his men's regard for him as they watched him eat. At five feet nine and 210 pounds, he was an imposing figure to his blooded followers. The thick, powerful body was the result of a *campesino*'s bonding between his mother and father during a midday's siesta. His face was a rich coffee brown, with thick, full lips and heavily hooded eyes. A huge Pancho Villa–inspired moustache gave him a sinister yet appealing air, one he carefully cultivated, knowing full well its effect on the women who were drawn to him. He wore his hair longer than most of his fellow officers, its blackness a reflection of his soul's empty pit. But it was the jagged bolt of raw, unbridled energy that truly captivated those who knew Melendez. He was a slave to his work, a zealot in its execution, a fanatic who knew no bounds when it came to crushing his enemies.

Above all, he considered himself a professional.

Stuffing a spoonful of beans and rice into his mouth, the major watched with interest as the last group of those arrested the night before were pushed, kicked, and shoved into a large cage made up of cyclone fencing. Slamming the steel mesh gate shut, a skinny *Guardia Nacional* corporal then snapped closed a heavy padlock which ensured that there would be no escape. Buried beneath the jittery mass of humanity was a platter charge consisting of ten pounds of C-4 plastic explosive. In just a few moments, Melendez would personally detonate the huge mine, a method of mass destruction he called "the Mixer."

Melendez spotted Ricardo Montalvo and his family, and decided to pay his last respects. As the headhunter made his way across the killing ground, Montalvo watched him, his face a mask that betrayed no emotion. Stopping within several feet of the cage, Melendez spoke. "Ah, Señor Montalvo. How gracious of you and your family to attend our little gathering today. I trust you are comfortable?"

Ricardo Montalvo pulled his wife and teenage daughter closer, his arms around their shoulders like a falcon protecting its nest. Considered by many of his countrymen to be La Libertad's only possible salvation from the rule of Colonel Aguilar, Montalvo was both respected and popular. So much so that the colonel had ordered his arrest and murder. Now, huddled together and sure of his family's fate, Montalvo was revolted by the pig who stood before him. "You will be made to account for this butchery, Major," he replied. "Sooner or later the United States will begin to investigate the outcry coming from the people, and when that happens there will be nowhere for you, or the bastard who sits in the capital, to hide."

Melendez nodded slowly, then launched a runny gob of spit directly into Montalvo's angry face. Resting his hand on the butt of his holstered Sig, the major ground his words out through tight lips. "Fuck you and the United States, you stinking Communist bastard! We can no longer tolerate the likes of you and your whores in La Libertad. All you do is protract the war with your idiot's words about freedom and democracy. This is *our* country, and we will see it bloom again by burying you and your kind whenever possible!"

Montalvo laughed as Melendez's spit ran down his cheek. "You call me a 'Communist,' Major? What you and your baboons have done here today reflects the same suppressive tactics used by the Russians and Chinese to eliminate their enemies! You may spit in my face, but I will spit on your grave when the time comes, and it is coming!"

Both men stared hard at each other, only the wire's barrier keeping them from trying to tear each other's throats out. Slowly, a smile began to erupt on Melendez's face. Eyeing Montalvo's daughter, he once again spoke. "You have a beautiful child, Ricardo. A woman, really. A shame one with so much to offer a man should be wasted before having the chance to experience one of life's greatest pleasures."

Montalvo's wife uttered a wail as she heard the oily words spoken, clutching the teenage girl to her in an iron grip. "Leave her alone, you pitiless swine," whispered Montalvo. "Kill us and the rest who suffer your arrogance, but do so quickly and without resorting to threats which have no meaning."

"You question my meaning, you whose daughter is now mine to use as I please? We have time, my impatient friend. Time enough for every man here to enjoy this sweet morsel while you and your subversive supporters watch!" Spinning on his heels, Melendez shouted at several jackbooted soldiers who were squatting under a tree. Leaping to their feet and grabbing their M-16 rifles, the men began to run toward their commanding officer, whose fury at being kept waiting was legendary.

Melendez turned again toward Montalvo, whose fingers were gripping the fence like claws, his face twisted beyond recognition as he realized what his prodding of the commando officer would now cost his daughter. "Please, please don't do this thing," he gasped.

"You should have considered your words before speaking them, you stupid bastard. Besides, once I am finished with . . . what is the girl's name . . . Maritza . . . yes, I'm sure that's it. Once I have enjoyed her, I will give her to my boys. They've worked hard today; killing is no easy task, you know. I'm sure their antics will be entertaining for you and your comrades."

Staring into the cage, Melendez only then noticed the hatred aimed his way from the eye sockets of those whom he planned to kill. Deep inside, he shuddered at their intensity, then, regaining his composure, he turned to order the girl's rape.

Melendez's words caught in his throat as the soldier nearest him had his head split open by a high-velocity round. The man's eyes bounced off the shocked major's chest, then dropped onto the sun-baked earth at his feet. "Sniper!" screamed Melendez as he threw himself to one side, avoiding a second bullet which struck one of the unfortunate prisoners inside the cage. From high up on the ridge surrounding them came the heavy drumbeat of a machine gun's deadly rhythm. The *whoosh* of an RPG-7 ended with the rocket striking Melendez's jeep, blowing his driver to hell and destroying any means of radio contact with the garrison seven kilometers away from El Refugio.

Melendez's men scurried for cover as a second machine gun opened up opposite the first. Crawling as quickly as he could, the major headed for the stand of boulders where his field desk sat, the hand-held detonator which would vaporize Montalvo and company sitting atop a tailored field jacket. Rifle fire began picking its way into the ragged perimeter formed by the death squad. Unable to coordinate a defense, each man fought as best he could against the still-unseen enemy, knowing full well that in defeat there would be no mercy from the guerrillas.

A second rocket slammed into the lava bowl, sending sharp bits of volcanic shrapnel flying. Melendez winced in pain as a golfball-sized chuck of rock smashed into his forearm, numbing it from the elbow down. He was less than thirty meters away from the desk, its squat shape barely visible in the dust and smoke that was becoming thicker with every detonation. A long string of machine-gun fire walked across his immediate front, coming to an end by burrowing a twelve-inch zipper into the stomach and chest of the same corporal who had secured the killing cage moments before. Melendez knew he had only seconds to get out of the gunner's sights if he was to reach the detonator in time.

Leaping to his feet, the burly major ran. All around him the air was abuzz with the sounds of battle. Grenades were erupting at the entrance to the bowl, a sure sign that his three-man position was locked in close combat with the guerrillas. As he dodged around one of his soldiers, whose leg was missing above the knee, Melendez had to acknowledge that the enemy commander knew his stuff. They were in a perfect horseshoe ambush, and with two machine guns firing he knew his troops were facing two platoons of guerrillas in the hills.

A massive explosion lifted Melendez high into the air, driving him forward as if he had been swatted by a giant's hand. Crashing into the ground, he rolled several feet and then lay dazed. Although now closer to his desk, which somehow remained undamaged, Melendez could not move. The concussion from the RPG's blast had deafened him, and he could feel thin rivulets of blood pouring from his nose and ears. Running a hand over his chest, he discovered that the expensive shoulder holster and gun were gone, victims of the blast. The knife was still in place, though. Hoisting himself up onto his hands and knees, Melendez shook his head back and forth, his senses somewhat restored. Gazing toward the cage, he could see the pile of humanity that was still within its confines. They had simply dropped to the ground, seeking the comfort of each others' bodies as if somehow their pathetic effort would defeat the steel flying through the air. Fools, he thought to himself. A few more feet and I'll send you all to hell!

Crawling on his hands and knees like a child, Melendez covered the remaining distance to his desk. Keeping his head down, he ran his hand along its surface, searching for the hard plastic detonator. Finding it, he snatched his hand back just as a heavy-caliber rifle round splintered the spot where the device had lain. Rolling to his right, he buried himself behind the small formation of boulders and checked the blaster's battery pack. Satisfied, he activated the detonator just as the guerrillas began their assault against the battered perimeter, now held by a handful of soldiers.

"Quickly, quickly now," urged Montalvo to his wife and daughter. When the firing had begun, they immediately dropped to the ground, thinking that Melendez had ordered his troops to begin the killing frenzy. They had watched with open mouths as the firefight unfolded, Montalvo slapping his hand against the ground every time a Guardia butcher was hit. Realizing that this was their only chance to escape, Montalvo pushed his arm underneath the cyclone fencing and retrieved the rifle which had fallen within reach when the first soldier was struck by the sniper's round. Ignoring his pain as the cage's sharp points ripped at his exposed skin, Montalvo pulled the weapon, an American M-16, back into the cage and turned its lean snout toward the padlock. Pulling the trigger several times, he blew the lock away, opening the door to freedom with a kick that sent it flying.

Pushing his family through the portal, Montalvo turned and faced the rest of the group now huddled on the ground. Even as he urged them to make a run for it, he knew they would not. They were like sheep, frightened beyond coherent thought by the vision of perdition before them. Clutching his wife closely to his side, Montalvo nodded his head toward the opening of a small arroyo just behind the cage. His daughter, eyes blazing with courage, returned his nod and began running. Montalvo waited only long enough to pull an extra magazine for the rifle from the dead soldier's combat harness, then followed.

Melendez quickly assessed his situation. His troops were no match for the guerrillas, and no doubt most of them were dead by now. He no longer heard the steady staccato of the machine guns, their silence meaning that the "G's" were too close to his own position for the enemy gunners to continue firing without hitting their own men. Indeed, rifle and submachine-gun fire seemed to be everywhere, with an occasional grenade detonating in the background. If he was to survive, he would have to go on the offensive. But how? Staring hard at the deadly black box in his hand, he recognized his only chance, and grinned.

Chancing a bullet between the eyes, Melendez shot a quick look toward where his desk still stood. The MP5 was still propped against it, a canvas bag full of loaded magazines next to the extended stock. He had a weapon now, if only he could live long enough to get to it. Melendez prayed for his men's resistance to cease; he needed the guerrillas to feel their victory within hand, and hopefully to become overconfident in their success.

Minutes later his prayers were answered.

Lying flat on his belly, Melendez edged his way forward so that he could observe the clearing where the guerrillas were bunching up. Here and there he could hear individual shots being fired as the "G's" cleaned house. Those not involved were raising their weapons in victory, huge smiles on their faces as they cheered each other on. Suddenly one of the men gave an order. Quickly obeying, the guerrillas began to move toward the cage where the prisoners still lay, despite their apparent salvation.

Just a few more steps, you Communist bastards, thought Melendez. It was obvious the attack was meant to free Montalvo, proving he was, as the colonel had said, a Marxist revolutionary hiding behind the mask of democracy just as Ortega had done in Nicaragua. Well, in a few short moments they would have their just reward, courtesy of Major Luis Melendez.

When the first guerrilla reached the open gate, Melendez depressed the thumb-sized button on his detonator. For an instant nothing happened. Then the ground erupted in a huge fireball as the enormous platter charge exploded. With enough force to bring down a ten-story building, the charge easily vaporized all those within its immediate range. Others who were still involved in the mop-up operation were thrown violently to the ground, or killed by the three tons of debris that flew through the air in every direction. Melendez himself was bounced several feet off the ground as the blast rolled over him. Sheltered by his rocky refuge, he sustained no new injuries.

Without waiting to inspect the ghastly results of his ambush, Melendez hurdled the stone outcropping and swept up the MP5 with its bag full of magazines. Zigzagging away from the clearing, he made for a small path which he knew would take him into a hidden ravine. From there he could make his way to the highway several klicks to the east, and flag down the first vehicle he encountered. Just as he was about to enter the ravine, a teenage guerrilla suddenly appeared on his right flank with a rifle in hand. Spinning to face the sentry, Melendez squeezed off half the subgun's magazine in a silent stream of steel-jacketed lead, which tore the boy nearly in two when it struck. Certain he had broken out of the guerrillas' outer security ring, Melendez quickly changed magazines and headed up the ravine.

• • •

Ricardo Montalvo ordered his wife and daughter to stop and rest for a moment. Turning to face his rear, he listened to the continuing gunfire, certain that they had made good their escape. As his wife tried desperately to catch her breath, Maritza moved to her father's side and began to bandage his still-bleeding arm with a strip of soiled cotton cloth torn from her blouse. Looking at each other, they smiled.

"You shoot well, *mi papa*," she said.

"Accuracy born of fear, my dear. I only wish our Holy Mother of God had seen fit to give me a shot at that vulture Melendez."

Behind them they heard the sounds of combat dying down. Then near silence. "Perhaps the guerrillas have finished the beast and his assassins off?" whispered the girl.

"Perhaps," responded Montalvo. "But we will not return to find out. There is a village near here where I have friends. We'll go there. If the guerrillas want us, they'll have to find us. In the meantime I'm afraid that our lives in La Libertad are over for the time being."

The girl was about to reply when the reverberation of a huge explosion caused them to hit the dirt. Gazing upward, they could see only a spiral of smoke and dust left by the massive detonation. "What was that, Papa?"

Grimly, the elder Montalvo answered his terrified daughter. "I'm afraid that was Major Melendez's grand finale for the day's butchery. Now we must go, in the memory of those who have just died." Hefting the lightweight assault rifle, he carefully lifted his still-weeping wife to her feet, and headed west, away from the smoking hell of El Refugio.

CHAPTER
2

Thornton eased his way along the narrow, leaf-strewn trail. Above him, the sun's rays punched themselves through the tree-tops, beams of hard white light striking the ground around him with the intensity of a minigun's burst. Stopping, he slowly slid his eyes from side to side, then listened closely to the sounds around him. Assured that he was still alone, the former Green Beret continued his recon.

The trail he was on dipped down into a natural depression, then looped its way upward to the ridge's crest. From there it ran the length of the mountain's wooded spine, intersected along the way by other trails and paths, forming a spider's web of natural highways throughout the coastal mountains. This particular trail ran through Thornton's property, land he'd recently bought and on which he was building his home. The five-acre purchase overlooked the craggy Oregon coastline and jutted deeply into the thickly wooded hills standing an impassive watch over Thornton's secluded domain.

It had been during a previous exploration of his holdings that he'd discovered the illegal marijuana plot growing below the ridgeline. He hadn't disturbed it just then, knowing its landlords would have set out crude booby traps to discourage intruders. Pot was Oregon's primary cash crop, and stories ran rampant about vast wilderness fields, tilled and guarded by professional dope farmers.

This trip, Thornton had come prepared.

He was wearing a worn, but serviceable pair of tiger fatigues which molded to every muscle and contour of his body as if they had been airbrushed on. Pulled down low on his forehead sat a similarly patterned boonie hat, its brim cut back to allow minimum protection from the elements without hindering his field of vision. His boots were made of thick rubber and canvas, their tops ending just below his knees. He wasn't wearing face paint.

Snuggled into a black nylon shoulder holster was Thornton's replacement for his recently retired Browning Hi-Power. The S&W 645 normally carried a combat load of nine rounds, but Thornton had customized his magazines so that they now held nine heart-stoppers in the rack, with a tenth in the tube. The stainless-steel automatic was impervious to the salty, wet coastal weather, and had a custom-quality double-action trigger, something the Browning lacked.

Strapped to his back was a small jungle ruck, its cramped interior filled with a bag of salt, some dried food, and two one-quart canteens. Tied onto the right side of the ruck was the AMK Pathfinder, a gift from Calvin Bailey, who called it a "Weed Whacker." Thornton smiled briefly at the thought of the DEA agent's choice of words; most appropriate, considering what he would be doing with the wicked twenty-one-inch reverse-curve blade over the next few hours.

Finally, hanging securely from his side, was the ever-present Randall 2 stiletto. Freshly honed and newly sheathed, the Randall had been with him since 'Nam, its razor-edged blade the veteran of a half-dozen close combat encounters. The last man Thornton had cut the life out of discovered the eight full inches of hand-forged steel deep within his guts after he'd tried to break Thornton's neck. Stennmaker lived long enough to feel his balls ripped from their comfortable sac before dying at Thornton's feet.

But retired Master Sergeant Beaumont "Bo" Thornton wasn't thinking of the former SEAL's field-expedient emasculation. He had other concerns at hand.

Ten feet ahead of him, he could see the beginning of the dope field. Slowly lowering himself to one knee, he felt a small depression form in the damp earth as he settled down to observe his objective. Within minutes, he located the first trap. Whoever had rigged it was obviously an amateur, as he'd chosen to cut his camouflage rather than use living foliage to hide his work. The dull green of the dead plants contrasted sharply with the vividness of the living, allowing Thornton to pinpoint the exact position of the device.

Continuing his visual recon, Bo confirmed there were no other traps set around or above the first. Crawling on his hands and knees, he moved to the base of a tall pine and stopped. Carefully tugging away several small branches and bits of moss, Thornton uncovered the crude but effective booby trap. It consisted of a twelve-gauge shotgun round fitted into a plywood base. Poised beneath the primer was a small nail which acted as the firing pin, a compressed, heavy steel spring wrapped around it. An equally tiny fishing hook barely held the spring in check, a trip wire adjusted so that when an unexpected visitor stumbled into it, the spring would be released, driving the nail against the primer, thereby detonating the round.

Thornton nodded his head in admiration of the designer's use of birdshot rather than buck. A wounded man would require immediate medical attention and would be moved. A dead man, on the other hand, would initiate both a police investigation and search of the area. Something dope growers didn't cotton to when it came to high-priced bud. Anyone setting off this particular trap would probably receive nothing more than a good scare, causing them to unass the AO without a thought of the police in mind.

Slipping a thick piece of tree bark between the round's primer and the hand-fashioned firing pin, Thornton deactivated the device. Extracting a battered pair of wire snips from his cargo pocket, he then cut the trip wire where it was knotted to the fishhook, rendering the trap harmless. Satisfied with his work, he slipped a placard the size of a playing card from his breast pocket, tacking it securely to the tree, just above the booby trap. Emblazoned on the card's white face was a black skull and crossbones. Printed above the leering death's head were the letters DEA, below, the phrase "It's A Way of Life." The cards were another gift from Calvin, who had adapted them from a similar one his SEAL team had used in Central America.

Knowing there were other similar traps present, Thornton spent the next hour working his way around the field's perimeter. In all, he found seven more shotgun devices and four strings of small bells, meant more as early-warning systems than anything else. Upon dismantling each gadget, he left one of the DEA cards, knowing that its presence would scare the living shit out of whoever returned for the harvest.

Satisfied that he could continue without having to worry about his own safety, Thornton lay his ruck against a fallen tree and removed the long-bladed Pathfinder from its sheath. For the next forty-five minutes he worked his way across the heavily forested patch, cutting each plant off just above its base, leaving the stalks where they fell. He estimated he'd whacked nearly one hundred fifty plants by the time he finished, the sweat from his efforts turning the camouflage shirt nearly black.

Conducting a quick recon of the perimeter, he returned to his ruck and removed the twenty-pound bag of salt he'd brought with him. Opening it, he moved through the field of fallen pot, sprinkling handfulls of salt over the carefully tilled soil. With the next coastal rain the ground would be poisoned, a mute reminder to any future drug growers of what they could expect if they continued to use Thornton's land for their plantations.

Gathering his gear, Thornton glanced at the heavy Rolex on his wrist. If he humped hard he would be back in time to meet Linda, who was taking him to lunch that afternoon. He'd spent the better part of the week working on his back deck, finishing it the day before. Now he had a place to stay as work on the house progressed, an eagle's view of the Pacific the reward for his efforts.

Still cautious, his wartime recon instincts alive and well, he checked his map and shot an azimuth west. It would be hard going for nearly seven hundred meters, but according to the map he should hit a fire trail which would lead him directly back to where he'd hidden his jeep. Shrugging into the rucksack, Thornton again surveyed his early morning's work, then vaporized into the surrounding bush.

Two hours later he wheeled the ancient four-wheel-drive rig into the gravel driveway of his new home. The bulletlike Corvette was already there, meaning Linda was waiting nearby. Stepping out of the vehicle, he watched as she appeared from a stand of fir screening the house's foundation.

As she made her way over the unpaved ground, Thornton again noted her beauty. Hers was a classic face, framed in a waterfall of auburn hair that hung below her sculpted shoulders in thick, wavy handfuls. Marvelously endowed, her figure possessed an erotic flow that even now was causing anticipation. They had met while he was vacationing, she working at the resort where he'd taken an apartment for several weeks. After the conflagration at Alpine, he once again retreated to the coast, sharing his life as well as his bed with her.

Now they were inseparable. Thornton, still amazed that after all his years alone he could fall in love, had never felt so complete.

Stepping up to him, Linda wrapped her arms around his damp neck and pulled his face down to hers. Giving him a kiss that was both heartfelt and teasing, she released him, standing back and frowning at his appearance. "Did someone give a war and not invite me?" she asked.

Pushing the boonie hat back, Thornton grinned. "Naw," he replied, "I was just checking the property line and decided to do some hiking up on the back ridge. Thinking of putting in a lean-to in case I want to do some hunting when the season opens."

"Looks to me like you were doing some hunting already," she observed. "As many times as I see that gun and knife of yours, I'm still not used to them. Blame it on my liberal background, and God help me if Mom ever finds out you were a Green Beret."

They both laughed, Thornton slapping her on the ass as she playfully grabbed his crotch. "You carrying a concealed weapon, or are you just happy to see me?" she teased.

"I thought you were taking me to lunch, young lady," he said with mock seriousness.

"I may have you for lunch if you don't settle down, Mr. Bo! Now order that cannon of yours to 'at ease,' and let's get back to town. I've got reservations for one-thirty, and if we take the 'Vette, we just might make it."

As Thornton guided the sports car through the winding turns of the coastal highway, Linda filled him in. She'd stopped by his apartment at the Breacon, checking the desk for any phone messages and grabbing the handful of mail that was in his box. Thornton listened to her as she read a letter from David Lee, who had recovered from his wounds and was now running Thornton's old A-team down in Central America. There was a note from

Frank, Thorton's partner at the Heavy Hook Dive Shop, and the expected assortment of bills.

"So much for the literate side of the house," Thornton commented. "Any calls?"

The girl sifted through the pile of paper in her lap, finally discovering the single call that had come for Thornton the day prior. "Calvin Bailey called yesterday. This says he'll try again today, but if he doesn't catch you, you're to call him as soon as possible."

Thornton glanced sideways at the vast expanse of ocean beach that was sliding past the Corvette's open window at seventy miles per hour. There weren't many people out, despite the warmth of the day. The beach, like his life up to this point, was fairly uncluttered and simple. The call from Bailey could change that, he mused.

"You want to cancel lunch?"

Thornton, turning his attention once again to the girl, shook his head in the negative. "No. But let's modify our plans a bit. How about picking up some sandwiches and soup while I shower, and we'll eat on the balcony. Okay?"

Linda pursed her lips before answering him, a pause hanging heavy in the Corvette. "Yeah, I suppose that's okay. You going to call Calvin while I'm out?"

"More than likely," he responded. Her question was expected. After all, she'd heard most of the story about Alpine and knew the major players, at least by name.

"Well, tell him hello for me, and if he's got another Mission from Hell for you, make sure the money is better than the last time. We only trust in God, everyone else pays cash."

Thornton laughed. "You're turning into quite the mercenary, aren't you?" he said. "I don't know if my hanging around has been the kind of influence your parents would approve of. . . ."

Linda grabbed him hard around the knee, causing his foot to leap off the gas pedal, banging hard against the bottom of the cushioned dash. "I'll worry about my virtue, thank you very much. You just get cleaned up, filled in, and ready to eat. If you're lucky, I may just show you a few things I *know* my parents wouldn't condone."

"Is that a promise or a threat?" growled Thornton as the Brea-con Point Resort spilled into view.

"Whichever you can handle best, stud."

Bo covered the last two miles to the hotel in record time, lunch forgotten as her lips brought him to the rigid position of attention.

CHAPTER

3

"Fuck me to tears, Thornton!" DEA agent Calvin Bailey pleaded into the phone's mouthpiece. "Please, *please* stop fucking with me every time I leave a damned message for you to call."

At the other end, Thornton chuckled at the hapless agent's frustration. Kicking the pile of dirty fatigues away from him so that they flew across the bedroom floor, he dropped into a thickly cushioned chair, propping his bare feet up on the end of the rumpled bed. "Easy, Cal, easy. It was just a little joke. How was I supposed to know you were hustling blowjobs from some Georgetown babe over dinner?"

"They say lightning never strikes twice, they say that, Bo." Bailey grabbed a handful of extension cord and stomped across his living-room floor. Outside his apartment, the lights of the Capitol burned hard against the remaining haze of the day. "Jeez, Bo. Ya gotta give me a break—you're killin' my sex life. Can't you call and leave a simple little message like everybody else?"

At the mention of Bailey's sex life, Thornton couldn't help basking in the warm glow of his own. Linda, quickly showering after an hour of atomic-grade lovemaking, was at the deli picking up their late lunch. Hearing the helpless tone in his friend's voice, the former recon artist who was Springblade's team leader couldn't help but twist the knife one more time. "Hey, if it'll help, I'll tell you about *my* sex life. It's been pretty damn good lately, and you'd appreciate some of the really bizarre things we've been doing to each other. . . ."

Bailey sat down hard on one of his K-Mart-special barstools, hanging his head in wretched defeat. "Okay. You win, you nasty

19

Army bastard. Tell me, tell me everything. Especially the part where you coat your tongue with—"

Now it was Thornton's turn to explode in laughter. "Whoa, I mean whoa, boy. Let's drop the subject and get to why you wanted to talk to me. Shit, Linda hear me sharing our private moments with a Mod-one class-A pervert like you, and I'd be floggin' my dong solo for the next month."

"Serve you right, too. I'm DX'ing this voice recorder-beeper bullshit and drawing something more conventional. Fuck me to tears, Thornton. Karen was a class act, too."

"That means she's outta your league, Skippy. So what's the poop? You and Billings got something cooking again?"

Bailey propped himself up on his elbows, wishing he'd stopped on the way back from the office to pick up some smokes. Eyes roving, he made the rounds of the ashtrays scattered around the room, pissed at himself for cleaning them before leaving for work that morning. "Hey, you gotta smoke I can bum?"

"Huh? A smoke? What the hell are you talkin' about, squid?"

"Nothing, just collecting my thoughts. Anyhow, the Man wants to know if you're available for a hop n' pop to San Francisco within twenty-four hours. Same arrangements as last time: you fly, we buy."

Bo launched himself from the chair into the bed, Linda's sweet fragrance filling his lungs once more as he sank into the heavy quilt she'd spread after they'd finished mauling each other. Pulling one of the huge bedroom pillows up under his head, he answered. "I dunno, Cal. I've got the decking finished up at the house, Jason and I poured concrete last week, and that's gotta be checked every day, plus Dealer McDope is growing his own on my back forty. Unless the money is primo, and the mission short term—"

Bailey interrupted. "You got the scrambler there?"

"Yeah. Give me a minute to hook it up."

Thornton reached into one of his drawers and retrieved the scrambling unit, plunging the connecting cables into an attachment on his phone. Now their conversation was being electronically mixed and distorted by means of the DEA's Voice Disruption Device, or VDEE. Bailey had ordered one for Thornton, knowing that Springblade required secure voice capabilities for future operations. "You there?" whispered Thornton.

"Roger that, asshole," replied Bailey, who had found a half-smoked Marlboro on the floor behind his couch while Bo was dicking with the VDEE unit.

"Shoot."

Calvin settled himself on the couch, lighting the cigarette and sucking in a mouthful of stale tobacco smoke. It was his only serious vice, and he wondered if he'd ever quit. Built like a bull mastiff, Bailey was a religious weight lifter and had recently taken up the Japanese martial art of kendo. In the corner of his cramped bedroom was a handmade Hartsfield *wakizashi* which had cost the agent nearly three months' pay. But, as Mohammed had so wisely said, "The sword is the key of Heaven and of Hell." In Bailey's constantly violent world, *his* sword was the one that counted, and so he practiced five hundred cuts a morning in front of his mirror, in memory of the prophet's prudent advice.

Blowing a shaft of gray smoke upward, he began. "You ever go up-country to La Libertad when you were with the Seventh?" he asked.

"Only once," Thornton replied. "A real dump compared to Costa Rica or El Sal. Me and two field grades were supposed to conduct a survey of their radio-relay stations. Since they only had three sites, it was a quick trip."

"Well, the good colonel, Arturo Aguilar, still reigns supreme as the country's rightful president. The problem is that our government is receiving an increasing number of reports detailing major human-rights violations, and that these are being conducted by Aguilar's personal death squads." Snubbing the cigarette out, Bailey continued. "Our number-one has made it clear to their number-one that the U.S. will not tolerate another Somoza-style dictatorship, and has had State demand free elections within six months or . . ."

"Or we pull our aid, leaving the colonel and his boys to fight the guerrillas by their lonesome. And if I read my *New York Times* right, the bad guys are kicking ass after six years of playing the game," finished Thornton.

"Exactly."

"So what the hell does that have to do with me going to San

Francisco, AIDS capital of the world and not exactly my favorite town?"

"Several weeks ago, a middle-of-the-road politico by the name of Ricardo Montalvo escaped with his family from some butchers' field called El Refugio. With help from the underground, he was able to cross into Mexico, then the U.S., where his *cuates* ran him up the corridor to the City by the Bay." Bailey paused, grabbing a report he'd been given which detailed Montalvo's successful escape from Melendez.

"Once he hit town, representatives of his party contacted the State Department and asked for Ricardo and family to be granted asylum. State went ape-shit because Aguilar had reported Montalvo as being the brains behind a recent massacre of 'loyal' civilians, and issued a warrant for his immediate arrest. So now we've got him buried in a safe house, waiting on State's investigation of the charges."

Thornton lifted his leg and blew a long, hard fart toward the open bathroom door, pleased that Linda wasn't around to chide him about his barracks etiquette. "Does Aguilar know Montalvo is in San Francisco?"

"Naturally. State, as usual, is playing both sides. On one hand they know that in an internationally supervised election, Montalvo would win the presidency hands down. We'd like that because Ricardo is by nature a conservative socialist in the grand old style of Central American politics."

"In other words, he's acceptable because he's moderate, pliable, *and* friendly toward us."

"Right. The complication is that the colonel's warrant is a legal document, and as such requires any nation with diplomatic ties to La Libertad to fully cooperate. State is stalling Aguilar's request for extradition until they come up with a plan. In the meantime we've been asked to provide a team to watch over the little family while they're here."

"Who's on them now?" asked Thornton. It seemed like overkill, asking his team to baby-sit when State had access to other, less covert teams than his. Hell, even the FBI possessed a high-risk outfit that could do the job Bailey wanted.

As if reading his mind, Calvin responded. "State's got a Bureau HRT with them now. The problem is that they figure Aguilar to send in his hitters just in case we don't give back the football."

"There's more to this than what we're discussing, Cal. Whenever State gets involved, the shit gets weird. Hell, I was in El Sal when they seriously considered rigging the elections when it looked like 'Major Bob' was gonna beat Duarte. If State is asking for us, it means it's time to weld a boiler plate over one's ass."

Bailey sighed. He knew what Thornton meant, and worse, he agreed with the man. When Billings handed him the request and asked him to contact Bo, they'd both experienced a sense of dread about the Montalvo case. Billings explained that he'd been told only as much as State wanted him to know. That meant the rules would be made up as the game progressed, a definite no-win situation when it came to whoever's task it was to take point and draw fire.

Dragging the phone behind him, Calvin yanked a cold one from the fridge, popped the top with one hand, and swallowed a long draught from the can before continuing. "Shit, Bo. Fly down and meet with me. If you don't like the movie, you're free to turn down the contract. That's something we made sure they understood. You, and you alone make the decision as to Springblade's deployment."

"Yeah, I bet they loved hearing that, huh?"

"Fuck 'em. You know who Billings reports to, and so do they. King George likes his knights, but his Trojan Horses are his pride and joy. You won't get hassled if you decline, it'll be Billings that takes State's heat."

Sitting up, Thornton rummaged through a nearby drawer and pulled a pair of UDT trunks out. With the phone carefully balanced on his shoulder, he wiggled into them, then grabbed a black SOG T-shirt from the adjacent closet. Dressed, he let Bailey finish his sales pitch.

"Speaking of Billings, why are you meeting me instead of him? No offense, but this seems pretty high speed—low drag, the kind of gig Billings would want to ramrod himself."

Bailey scratched his balls, wishing it was the Georgetown fox's hand stuffed down his pants rather than his own. "Conrad took a thirty-eight slug in the calf about ten days ago. Crackhouse raid went sour, he was providing backup for another agent when one of the *brothers* popped out of a trapdoor in the ceiling. He managed to get off a shot, but Billings drilled him with a laser-mounted American 180 before the big bastard realized he'd been hit himself."

"He okay?" asked Thornton. Bo had met Billings in D.C. when Springblade was activated, instantly respecting the veteran DEA man. When Alpine went down, it was Billings who led the troops into the inferno after Thornton and his team had turned the place into a raging hell on earth. Conrad Billings was Thornton's kind of guy; he hoped the wound wasn't serious.

"Oh, yeah, the bullet passed right through, didn't expand worth a damn. They put him on two weeks' leave, although he comes in every day to 'visit,' and he'll be back on the streets by the time this Montalvo bullshit is over with."

Sitting back down on the bed, Thornton glanced at the clock, knowing that Linda would be back any minute with their food. He had a few more questions for Calvin before hanging up, though. "How many, how long, and how much?"

Bailey, now knowing Thornton would at least come to San Francisco, happily gave the big commando the information he wanted. "You can bring in the whole team, primarily because everyone speaks Spanish and we don't know how big a force Aguilar might send if State denies extradition. Billings was told you'd be on site no more than one week. After that, Montalvo will either be a guest of the United States government, or he'll be chum for one of the colonel's fishing trips. Give me your fee, and I'll present it to the Man."

Thornton grabbed a pencil and paper from the bedside table. Asking Calvin to hold for a moment, he did some quick figuring, then punched back into the line. "Fifteen hundred per man, per day. All expenses paid. Life insurance just like the last time out, don't forget the loss-of-limb clauses. Once a man steps onto the plane, he's paid for the week even if the mission's scrubbed while he's en-route. If we go past seven days, each man receives a twenty-five-hundred-dollar bonus for each additional week on the job, one day more equals a week. Got it, squid?"

"Highway motherfucking robbery . . . but not out of the question, considering the stakes. I'll pitch it and let you know ASAP. Anything else?"

Thinking of Lee's letter, Thornton realized that he might have to go in one man short, *if* he accepted the contract. That would mean having to work the Montalvos with a three-man team, or taking on a straphanger. Thornton didn't like working with someone he didn't know. He'd had straphangers, a term applied to paratroopers who tagged along on jumps they weren't originally manifested for, along on missions and it seemed they got zapped, or were the cause of someone else sucking up a round. There were exceptions, but they were men known to the teams they piggy-backed with, and proven in combat.

"Lee may be operational out of Task Force Bravo. If that's the case, we'll be going in shorthanded. I won't pull him away from his team regardless of how important this Montalvo character may be."

"I can dig it," answered Bailey. Calvin knew the importance of team integrity, especially during real-world deployment, when each man on a team had to think of mission accomplishment before himself. If Lee was indeed op-conned to TFB, he was running some serious business for the SouthCom commander. They'd have to find a replacement for him, one that Thornton would accept. "Let's talk first. In the meantime, I'll make some calls. There might be someone you know in one of our SLAM teams. If so, I'll run the name by you."

"If I don't like it, you may end up the pinch hitter yourself," warned Thornton, "and what the fuck is a SLAM team? Sounds like something we had during Nam."

Bailey thought about having another beer, then decided against it. "It stands for 'seek, locate, annihilate, and monitor.' Each team consists of six men, four teams make up a troop. We have three troops currently operational. One in Southeast Asia, one in South America, and one in the Middle East. Their only reason for living is to take our verified reports of drug traffic in these areas, and interdict using any means possible."

"These regular government types, military, or free lance?"

"They're all contract operatives, with the exception of the team leaders who are detached from either the NSA, CIA, or our own agency. Pretty successful program, too. High personnel turnover, though."

Thornton snorted into the phone. "I'll just fucking-A bet there is. If you find someone I know in one of those teams, just leave him there 'cause he's got to be a loony tune."

He was about to continue when he heard Linda's key in the door. "Hey, gotta go. Ring me back when you've got something firm, in the meantime I'll call Frank and Silver. Oh, one last thing, Cal . . ."

"Yeah?"

"Quit scratchin' your nuts. The sound drives me crazy!" With a laugh he switched off the scrambling unit, stowed it in the bottom drawer of his dresser, and hung up the receiver even as Bailey was screaming something about Thornton's depraved taste for young girls into the phone. Wandering out into the kitchen, he could smell the healthy aroma of fresh roast beef. Linda was already spreading a white linen tablecloth on the breakfast counter next to the open sliding glass door. She smiled as he caught her eye, and invited him to eat.

CHAPTER
4

San Francisco International was one of those airports Thornton enjoyed flying into. He'd spent more than one layover downing straight shots of Jack Daniels Black in one or another of the comfortable airport lounges, awaiting flights back to Bragg or Vietnam, whichever direction his orders read. That was a long time ago, he thought to himself as he and his fellow passengers waited for the ground crew to release them from their now-chaotic airliner. Now, everywhere he looked there were runways, terminals, and huge open-bay hangars. On a more sobering note, he saw the battered wrecks of more than one aircraft shoved off the ends of the tarmac, mute reminders of the danger of flying the friendly skies.

Breaking away from the stream of arriving passengers, he didn't bother looking for a welcoming committee. Bailey would be waiting for him on the other side of the security checkpoint, not wanting to draw attention to himself by having to flash his ID in order to get through with his gun. Thornton's own 645 rode comfortably under his leather flight jacket. His federal permit allowed him to carry it on board by simply filling out a form at the Alaska Airline counter in Portland. He still needed to claim his duffel bag from luggage, however. Should he accept the mission, he wouldn't have time to return to Cannon Beach for his things, so he'd packed what he needed and brought it with him.

Ignoring the pulsating masses, Thornton weaved his way toward the main terminal. He couldn't help but notice the servicemen in their dress uniforms, all involved in the military madness

27

of "hurry up and wait." As usual, the officers were either clus-
tered around a table comparing their last efficiency reports, or
heading for private host rooms scattered about the airport. The
enlisted men were content to wander through the gauntlet of
overpriced shops, or were attempting to catch some sleep while
they waited for their flights to be announced. A select few were
getting drunk, careful to avoid the stares of those officers who
never missed a chance to fuck with the troops if given half an
opportunity.

Thornton remembered the last rank-conscious son of a bitch
who'd decided to hassle him. As Bo remembered him, he was
one of those portly sorts who just had to have a finance MOS,
and was used to the fawning attention of administrative troops
who knew where their bread was buttered. A missed connection
had left young Staff Sergeant Thornton stranded, the next available flight to Hawaii not until zero-dark thirty the following
morning.

Major Disaster had bobbed his way into the lounge with several junior-grade officers in tow. Only one wore a combat patch
on the right shoulder of his neatly pressed jacket, Thornton remembered the way the 1st Cav patch stood out against the deep
green of the man's uniform. The officer, a captain, had an Airborne tab sewn above it. Not many of those bastards around, Bo
had thought. The First was airmobile, but it possessed the only
airborne-qualified company that had deployed to the Nam with
the mission of running long-range reconnaissance. If this captain
was one of those guys, chances were he wasn't a fuckup like the
rest of the major's ducklings.

The Green Beret hadn't exactly been out of uniform, but
Thornton did admit to himself that he had taken liberties. On his
right wrist was a solid copper band, given to him by the Yard
tribe he'd worked and lived with for six long months. The Rolex
graced his left wrist, and a heavy eighteen-karat Special Forces
ring was wrapped around his wedding finger. His uniform was
custom-tailored in Saigon, and he'd unbuttoned the jacket once
he'd entered the bar. The beret he was so proud of was upside
down on the bar, its issue liner replaced with one sewn from
parachute silk. In it he'd tossed his cigarettes, an engraved Zippo
lighter, some change, and a wad of spending money he'd been

paid for attending the condensed O&I course at Bragg.

For his own reasons, the tubby major decided to correct Thornton's appearance in front of his fellow officers. The lecture came to an immediate halt when Thornton grabbed the man by the back of the head, pulling him up hard against the blue-and-silver Combat Infantryman's badge Bo was wearing on his left upper breast. Burying the major's nose against it so that the officer was forced to breath through his mouth or suffocate, Thornton proceeded to explain the difference between combat troops and rear-echelon motherfuckers to the struggling blob of fat held securely in his powerful hand.

The captain stepped in just as Bo was planning to introduce the red-faced ROTC graduate's marshmallowlike butt to one of his spit-shined jump boots. Leading the babbling officer toward the rest room, the captain indicated with a casual hand-and-arm signal that Thornton might best find a hole until his flight left. Bo had returned the gesture with a thumbs-up of his own, and performed a disappearing act that would have made Houdini proud. As he sauntered past the remaining officers, he heard one of them whisper, "Shit, looka the ribbons the bastard's wearing! Fucking major is lucky to be alive. Special fucking Forces . . . what a trip!"

"How was your trip?"

Thornton snapped out of his daydream at Calvin's question, asked just as he was stepping past the rent-a-cop whose job it was to intercept international terrorists and detain them for questioning. The DEA agent wore Levis, snakeskin cowboy boots called "exotics" by the drug merchants he chased, and a tan sport shirt. His S&W .357 was hidden from view by a red-and-gold satin jacket, the emblem of the San Francisco 49'ers embroidered on its back.

"Fine," he answered. "I was just remembering the last time I was here. It's changed."

Bailey steered them toward the baggage-claim area, talking as they went. "No shit, how so?"

"Back in the sixties, San Francisco was the City of Love. Eric Burdon wrote a hit song about it, Bill Graham staged rock shows at Winterland, hell, even the Hells Angels chapter was somewhat mellow. I don't get the same feeling that I had when I was here last, just seems kinda empty."

Stepping off the escalator and reading a monitor directing them to Claim Area 5, Calvin noted the hint of sadness in the big man's voice. "Well, shit happens. All that's here now is the biggest community of cocksuckers and buttfuckers the good old U.S. of A. has to offer. On top of that you've got AIDS, ARC, Chinese gangs, black gangs, Latin gangs, dopers, hitmen, burned-out rock legends, and some of the best French bread on the West Coast. Maybe it ain't what it use da' be, but it's all we got."

Thornton, spotting his duffel bag, turned to his broadly smiling friend with a look of sour amusement. "Thanks, I feel a lot better now."

Bailey reached in front of a creature standing next to them who could have passed as either male or female, depending on the day of the week. Grabbing the heavy OD bag by one of the two shoulder straps dangling from it, he hefted the load easily off the luggage carousel and began heading toward the crowded exit. "Hey, that's my motto in life," he quipped as he pushed ahead of Thornton. Turning to wink at the man who ran the baddest covert-ops team in the league, he added, "If you can't say anything positive, then say the most negative thing that comes to mind."

His laughter was lost in the din of the airport's impossible traffic.

Richard Lippman stood in front of the ornate mirror, smoothing the lapels of his dark gray suit. Satisfied, he touched the blood red knot of his tie, then carefully inspected the positioning of his pearl tie-tack. At forty-five years of age, he was one of the youngest State Department troubleshooters in George Bush's administration. A career behind-the-scenes man, Lippman possessed a reputation for being absolutely ruthless in the execution of his assignments.

A graduate of Stanford, he'd entered government service immediately after attaining his degree. He learned quickly that power was a much better reward than public recognition, and sought positions that would allow him to become a part of the bigger State Department picture than those who liked to see their names in the papers. The most pivotal decision Lippman had made was the one to specialize in Central and South American affairs while his peers were flocking to classes on the Middle East. He'd become part of what was a struggling department in the early and mid-seventies, only to be acknowledged as an integral player when Ronald Reagan rode into power atop Jimmy Carter's political corpse.

Lippman was gracefully tall and tastefully lean. He was a moderate jogger, avid handball player, and occasional bird hunter. His face was both attractive and forgettable, a good combination for a man in his line of work. Lippman wore his light brown hair in a conservative cut, and was always clean-shaven.

He dressed according to the occasion, and with respect to whomever he was dealing with.

Today he was meeting two men whom he knew little to nothing about. State's orders were clear. The men represented a team whose existence was known to a very select and powerful few. One of the men was a DEA agent, the other an independent means to whatever end was necessary. He admitted to himself while crossing the room to where his briefing materials were arranged, that he had been startled when told that the second man, the independent, would have the final say as to whether he'd accept Lippman's assignment or not.

In twenty years of service, he'd never heard of such operational freedom being extended to an operative.

Seating himself, Lippman began again to digest what such a liberty might be translated as. First, it meant that the secretary had no influence with the president concerning the activities of this man. That meant he, whoever "he" was, reported directly to the Oval Office through a single conduit. If the DEA were providing an escort, it would be logical to assume that agency had more than just a casual association with the man he was supposed to convince to stay.

Lippman knew about covert operations. He'd been behind the scenes on more than one during his posting to the NSA, including the very successful support of the Contras. He'd been impressed by North's handling of that effort, and had met quite a few of the field players who'd carried out the actual missions. Lippman wondered if he might have met the man somewhere before, perhaps on a jungle landing strip along the Honduran border, or at one of the CIA stations in the gulf.

If his first assumption was correct, it meant that he was being entrusted with a secret which could benefit him in the future, *if* he played his cards right. That meant he needed to analyze this unknown player's capabilities and personality very quickly. Should he come on too hard, the man might well leave without a second thought. Lippman shook his head. That would not earn him any points in Washington. On the other hand, he couldn't come on like some bureaucratic wimp. Men who walked in the shadows despised politicians to begin with, and hated those who worked for them even more. Should he appear foppish, the man might kick his balls in and then leave, the situation still unresolved.

What the man from State really hated was the fact that he was finally meeting one of those chosen elite who could, based on how much he liked Lippman's upcoming performance, dictate his own terms. It was an uncomfortable feeling.

Then again, Richard Lippman enjoyed challenges. Should he "cut the mustard," as his father used to say, he would be privy to a circle so small that it awed even him. George Bush was no man's fool. His administration was as dedicated as the previous president's had been except that Bush was not an actor turned politician. He was a career power broker who had climbed the ladder with single-minded determination. Where Reagan had only nodded assent, Bush was willing to pull the trigger himself. Lippman could appreciate that kind of commitment.

Regardless of Montalvo's fate, Lippman needed to enlist the aid of this mysterious guest.

The sound of someone knocking on the door triggered his professional composure. Leaving the table, Lippman strode across the polished tile floor and invited his visitors in. After closing the door, he turned, held out his hand, and introduced himself. "Gentlemen. My name is Richard Lippman, and I am representing the interests of the secretary of state."

Bailey responded, his thick hand snaking out to grasp Lippman's in a respectful but firm grip. "Calvin Bailey, DEA. A pleasure to meet you, sir."

"Likewise," returned Lippman. "And . . ."

"This is Mr. Thornton," Bailey offered, making the introduction for both men. "He's been informally briefed by myself, but I don't think I've stolen any of your thunder, sir."

Lippman smiled. Thornton reached out and shook the hand of the man from State, their eyes locking onto each other's in an effort to read who the inner man might be, as opposed to what each was projecting outwardly.

"Thank you for the invitation, Mr. Lippman. It's been some time since I last enjoyed the opportunity of visiting San Francisco." Bo broke eye contact first. He'd seen what he needed to, and to have continued the visual tug-of-war would have been juvenile.

Lippman scored the first round to Thornton. A hardcase, he thought to himself. Very professional, diplomatic, and without the typical mercenary's "I'm bad" attitude. Lippman's mind hadn't missed the fact that Thornton had addressed him as an equal, where Bailey's use of "sir" showed that he regarded himself in the subordinate role. It was going to be an interesting day, Lippman mused.

Indicating the table where they'd be sitting, Lippman led the men across to it. After they'd pulled up their chairs, he ordered a plate of sandwiches and bottled water up from the hotel's kitchen. Both Bailey and Thornton noted to themselves that they hadn't been asked whether they were hungry, although both men were. Thornton watched Lippman carefully; he knew the man was working them like an actor does a crowd. And he was good, damn good.

After the food was ordered, Lippman stood and slipped his coat off, carefully folding, then laying it on the nearby sofa. Once again, seated, he picked up an eight-by-eleven color photo of Ricardo Montalvo, and passed it directly to Thornton. Without waiting for Bo's reaction, Lippman began.

"Ricardo Montalvo is the most dangerous political rival Colonel Arturo Aguilar has to contend with in La Libertad. He is a socialist moderate who was educated in both the United States and France. His popularity with the masses is unquestioned and growing. To our knowledge he has not encouraged or participated in the guerrilla war being waged by Marxist forces in his country. They, on the other hand, are very aware of Montalvo and see him as a valuable tool for future use . . . should they win, of course."

"And will they?" asked Thornton.

Lippman leaned forward, pinching the bridge of his nose between his forefinger and thumb. "For six years the guerrillas have been waging a nearly perfect insurgency. They are reaching the final stage, where they will be both willing and able to carry out prolonged conventional military operations against Aguilar's forces. It is State's opinion at this time that, yes, the insurgency will topple the colonel's government."

A knock at the door informed them that the food had arrived. Bailey volunteered to bring it in, Lippman giving him a friendly nod. With just the two of them at the table, Thornton posed his most important question to Lippman. The man's answer would either keep him at the table or head him out the door. He didn't want to waste his time playing political "Wheel of Fortune" with a man whose motives Thornton would never really know.

"Why bring me in? Bailey says you have the Montalvos covered by an FBI team, and if you don't think they're good enough, there's a smorgasbord of antiterror units you could replace them with."

Lippman felt the verbal gauntlet land between them. Warp factor ten, Mr. Lippman, he thought to himself. You're going to be eating lunch alone if you don't grab this bastard by the balls in the next thirty seconds. And when you've got them by the balls, their hearts and minds will follow, he reflected.

"Aguilar has charged Montalvo with the murder of fifty loyal citizens. He also claims that Montalvo was actually on site when the killings took place, and that he gave the final order for the killing to begin." Lippman paused to gauge Thornton's response to this, then continued.

"Aguilar claims the guerrillas smuggled Montalvo out of the country. In fact, it was Ricardo's political supporters that got him to San Francisco, just ahead of the colonel's most able assassins. Once Aguilar discovered the bird had flown the coop, he issued an arrest warrant to the international community."

Bailey returned, a plate for himself and Thornton in his hands. "I'd have put something together for you, sir, but I didn't know whether you liked baloney or ham . . . in your sandwiches that is."

Lippman smiled. "Actually, I prefer turkey, Mr. Bailey. If

you'll excuse me for a moment, I'll be right back and we can continue as we eat." Without waiting for either man's approval, Lippman retreated to the buffet counter.

Thornton glanced at Bailey, then tore a huge bite from his sandwich. Talking as he chewed, he advised Bailey to take it easy with the State Department official. "You still work for these assholes, Cal. Fuck with this guy too much, and I'll double-damn guarantee you'll regret it. I've seen his kind in Vietnam and in Central America. They order guys like you and me to go where no man has been before, then forget us as soon as the political goal has been accomplished."

Bailey nodded. "Yeah, you're right. No sense boiling my own nuts. Hey, you know what the clerks and jerks call Lippman behind his back?"

Thornton shook his head.

"Dick Lips! They call him Dick Lips. Can you dig that?"

"So?" responded Thornton, unsure of what Calvin was driving at.

"So? So can you imagine how many guys in this city would *love* to have a nickname like that?"

Thornton choked on a piece of roast beef, then managed to slide it down his throat with the help of half a bottle of water. Turning to his friend, he wagged his right index finger slowly back and forth, then drew it across his throat.

At that moment Lippman returned, his plate full and his tie carefully loosened, the top button of his shirt open. "I trust the food is as good as it looks," he asked.

Both men nodded and waited for Lippman to start the briefing. He drew them out, taking his time by eating half a sandwich and most of his salad. Experience had taught him that soldiers—real soldiers—didn't like the breed of man Lippman represented. He knew he couldn't become their friend; that wasn't his goal or concern. What he wanted was Thornton's team in San Francisco until State decided what to do with Montalvo. He'd get them here, but on his terms and with his dignity intact.

Finishing his salad, Lippman began as if there hadn't been a ten-minute break in the conversation. "State has been monitoring the situation in La Libertad for some time now. In order to assure our continued role in the region, we've been sending enough support to Montalvo and his party to keep them afloat. At the same time, we've continued to support Aguilar, in case he is lucky enough to win the war."

Thornton pushed himself away from the table, staring hard at Lippman, who seemed to take no notice of his words' effect on the big bone-breaker. "In other words, you've been playing both sides against each other, and now Montalvo has his dick in a ringer—a ringer you created."

Lippman nodded.

"So what the fuck happens if State decides to keep Ricky-baby alive and well?" This time it was Bailey speaking. "I mean, won't Arthur and the boys be just a little pissed at Uncle Sam if we don't give this guy back?"

"State is checking into the allegations made by Aguilar. We don't believe them for a minute, but we have to put on a show as if we *might*. Should our analysis of the situation in La Libertad show that the colonel is on his way out, we will keep Montalvo here. Supervised elections are to be held in six months, and it is our assertion that Ricardo Montalvo will win them in a landslide vote. On the other hand, *if* the colonel makes some major concessions to the people, such as land reform, an end to the death squads, and so on, we may have to remit the Montalvos to him for trial."

"Heads we win, tails he loses. That's what you're saying, isn't it?"

Lippman returned both men's glares with an icy-cool one of his own. "That's correct, Mr. Thornton. Politics in Central America have a life of their own. Here in the U.S. we are children compared to how they play the game. Television decides our head of state for us. There, a bullet does. But both of you already know that. Your outrage is toward my seemingly callous attitude, not the situation itself."

"Fuck you . . . sir," exclaimed Bailey. "I spent some time down south myself, and this kind of thing sucks the big one in my book."

Thornton jumped in before Bailey could ruin his career with one more ill-advised shot at Lippman. Bo understood the reality of what Lippman was saying. He didn't like it, damn sure didn't condone it, but he fucking-A understood it. "*If* I bring my people in, what happens if State keeps Montalvo alive?"

Lippman stood, walking to an open window overlooking the city. Gazing out, he reminded himself of other cities in other countries, where he'd stood just like this, poised on the edge, wondering whether to step forward or back, and if it really made a difference either way. With his back to the two men, he replied, "If Montalvo stays, I will be escorting him back to the capital, where we'll salt him and his family away until the elections. Your people will only be responsible for the one week we feel he'll need to stay here. After that, another team will assume responsibility for their safety."

Thornton left his seat, striding quickly to the other man's side. For the briefest of moments, Lippman thought Thornton might push him through the open frame. He'd have shit if he'd known how acceptable the thought was in Bo's mind as he came to stand shoulder to shoulder with the political reptile, both men now staring hard out over the city.

"And what if *State* sends Montalvo *back*?" Bo hissed into Lippman's ear. "Where will you be? I've no doubts in my mind that you'll want us to drag Montalvo and his screaming family onto the first thing smokin' toward La Libertad. What I want to know is where the fuck you'll be if that happens . . . Dick Lips!"

Lippman turned slowly until he was nose to nose with the angry shadow warrior. Their eyes fused together fiercely in the firestorm of Thornton's majestic rage. For a moment Lippman let the silent hurricane within himself wreak havoc. No one called him Dick Lips to his face, although he knew the cowards in his office used the term whenever they felt he was out of earshot. Letting the fury of the insult beat itself to death behind his frozen mask, he broke eye contact with Thornton, evening their score. "If that decision is made by *State*, Mr. Thornton, I'll buckle the Montalvos into their seats and serve them dinner on their way back to Colonel Aguilar and his band of baby-killers. You have my word on that."

Thornton spun on his heels, signaling to Bailey that it was time to leave. As both men reached the door, Lippman, again looking out the window, stopped them with a final question. "When will I have *your* decision, Mr. Thornton?"

Bo turned, glaring at the man's back. His jaws were tight with the knowledge that Lippman had given him the one answer that would keep him in San Francisco. Thornton believed the man, he believed he would do just as he said, whichever way it went. That took guts, a trait Thornton respected above all others.

"You'll have my decision tomorrow morning at breakfast."

Lippman closed his eyes tightly, then opened them. "That'll be fine. Thank you for coming."

As the door slammed shut, Richard Lippman voted himself an Oscar for the best performance of his life.

CHAPTER

5

The sun was dipping below the ocean's farthest lip, its brilliant orange glow a fiery backdrop for the city's concrete spires and towers. Thornton sat alone on the balcony of the penthouse suite reserved for his and Bailey's use. They had returned to the hotel immediately after meeting with Lippman, an encounter that still rankled Thornton. Bailey, awake for the last thirty-seven hours, was asleep in his room, leaving Bo to himself. He was using the solitude to rehash everything Lippman had said, looking for ghosts in the shadows, as his mother used to tell him whenever he awoke from a bad dream.

The smooth sound of well-oiled rollers informed him that Bailey was awake. Without turning, he greeted the other man as he stepped through the glass door and onto the terrace. "You get enough sleep?"

Shaking his head from side to side to clear the last remnants of sleep from his consciousness, Bailey pulled a chair from under the petite breakfast table and joined Thornton, who was watching the waning sun's demise. "Depends what your definition of 'enough' is, I suppose," he answered. "Damned comfortable bed, though. One thing about State, they pull out all the stops when they want to impress you."

"Yeah, Lippman impressed the shit outta me. I gotta give it to the evil bastard, though; he's smooth as silk and cold as ice when it comes to selling people down the road." Thornton leaned over and grabbed the slim sheath knife that was lying next to his chair. Using it as one would a pointer, he punctuated his words as if he were a teacher in a classroom.

"Lippman comes from the old school, the school that teaches you to smile as you kill. If I bring the boys in, we'd better feel our assholes pucker when needle-dick starts lickin' and grinnin' around us."

Bailey began laughing. "Fuck me to tears, Bo. When you called Lippman Dick Lips, I near shit my pants. I don't think *anybody* has had the nuts to call him that to his face." Small tears were forming in the corners of the narc's eyes, his laughter forcing Thornton to smile in spite of his attempt not to.

"You gotta hand it to him," Bo marveled. "He kept his shit in one bag. I figured that would blow his act wide open, but he played right through it. Fuckin' guy won't forget me, though . . . guys like that never forget you once you've pulled their pants down in front of the world."

"Yeah? Well fuck him and the horse he rode in on," snorted Bailey. Looking at the knife in Thornton's hand, he pointed a finger at it. "Hey," he said, "what kinda blade you packin' now? I don't recall seeing that one our last time on the road together."

Bo pulled the lean piece of hand-ground steel from its nylon sheath, carefully handing it to Calvin, who blew a low whistle of approval at its balance and symmetry. The knife was nine inches long, five of those inches a perfectly ground double edge. The handle boasted a full tang with back micarta scales, a slim double guard present to keep one's fingers from sliding onto the blade during a thrust.

Bailey was impressed.

"This is one lean, mean killin' machine. Where'd you pick it up?"

Accepting the blade, Thornton neatly palmed it in one light-ning-quick motion. The last rays of the sun bounced off of the double hollow grind, reminding Bailey of Aztecs, Incas, and sac-rificial hearts.

"Cuban I met in Honduras. He's one of those guys who's been around since the Bay of Pigs, doin' the Agency's contract work whenever and wherever it may be. When I met him he was run-nin' boats against the Nics, arms intercept, shit like that.

"We were drinking downtown one night with a buncha his naval commandos, really partying it up 'cause they'd captured a load of M-16s comin' across the gulf. We later found out the guns were *supposed* to still be in Vietnam.

"Anyhow, this Honduran paratrooper who'd wandered into the party started talkin' shit about how the Airborne was so much fuckin' better than the 'ducks,' as Tio's boys were called. Well, old Tio goes over and tries to calm things down before the shit hits the fan, and the trooper pulls a big K-Bar on him.

"Quicker than poop comin' outta a big brown goose, Tio whips this mean little fucker outta some kinda sheath he's got on his forearm. He slaps the K-Bar away as the trooper comes at him, then wraps his left arm around the kid's head like this. . . ."

Standing, Thornton demonstrated the scene for Bailey, his left arm wrapped around an imaginary head, the right hand holding the dagger just in front of his chest.

"Anyway, Tio grabs this doomed bastard, twists his head sideways so he's got a bird's-eye view down this one big ear, then rams the fucking knife straight down the tube and into the brainhousing group.

"One second the para's struggling like a madman, the next he's a corpse on the floor. Tio slips his blade outta the ear hole, wipes it across the dead trooper's cloth jump wings, and sits back down as if nothin' has happened."

A long silence hung between the two men as Thornton finished the story. Finally, curiosity aroused, Bailey asked what happened after the fight ended.

"A coupla Hondo MPs showed up, Tio flashed some fuckin' badge he had, and they left us alone. Last I saw, they were draggin' the dead para facedown out the door. Never heard anything about it after that.

"When it came time to *di-di* back to Panama, Tio shows up right before the chopper is due, and hands me this knife. Said it was a gift, that he knew I appreciated good tools, and he wanted me to have it as a reminder of why paratroopers ain't shit."

Both men laughed, memories of past brawls between their two units over much the same thing rushing through their minds. Slipping the knife into its nylon home, Thornton glanced at his watch. Noting it was past six already, and remembering he and Bailey hadn't eaten since their meeting with Lippman, he suggested dinner.

Within minutes, both men were dressed and heading for the elevator. Thornton waited until they were on the sidewalk before asking Bailey about the oddly shaped walking stick he carried. As a cab cut across two lanes of evening traffic to pick them up, Calvin slapped the cane lightly against this outer calf. "It's something your friend Tio would appreciate," he said.

"Maybe," replied Thornton, ducking low into the cab's bright interior. "Two months after I left the country, his boat was blown outta the water during an exfil, they never found his body."

Bailey was silent as the cab driver expertly slewed his way back into traffic. A sign above the dash reminded them to use condoms while they were in town.

"Whatta we gonna do now, Turk?"

"Shut up, you little queen. I'm thinkin'."

"Well, honey, you'd better think fast," quipped a third voice, "'cause we're outta cash and the night is still young."

There were five of them altogether. Dressed in tight black leather clothing, with loops of silver chain hanging from their shoulders and hips, they might have looked like nothing more than bikers out for a night on the town. A closer look would reveal that these were not exactly your average Harley riders, though.

Turk, their leader, stood six four, without heels. Heavily muscled, he wore a tight yellow T-shirt under his six hundred-dollar motorcycle jacket. Instead of pants, he had on leather riding chaps and a pair of black bikini briefs, visible where the chaps were split in an open invitation. On each hand was a fingerless black leather glove. His boots, of the same material, were calf-high and severely pointed. Around each ankle was a heavy gold chain secured to a stirrup, whose star-shaped points had been carefully sharpened to a razor's keenness. Atop his head sat a proper English bowler, worn so that it rode low on his forehead, its narrow brim casting a demonic shadow over obsidian eyes.

The other men were dressed much the same way, but lacked Turk's flair. They were the hard core of San Francisco's gay community; rough sex was their religion, brutality their means of attaining it. Tonight they'd begun by snorting nearly a gram of premium methamphetamine apiece. The speed running through their systems was followed by a shared fifth of cheap whiskey taken from a still-unconscious drunk. They'd spent the last two hours at a bar called The Chocolate Highway, posturing for their friends and buying drinks for anyone that came in.

Now they were dangerously intoxicated, viciously wired, and broke.

"Girls," growled Turk, "we gotta score some bread in a hurry. Seems to me we might as well have a little fun while we're at it. Whatta ya think?"

Oboe, the meanest of the group, snapped a pair of nunchaku from under his vest. Whipping the ironwood sticks from side to side in a drug-induced frenzy, he lashed out at a nearby parked car, the 'chucks smashing through one of its windows in a shower of fragmented safety glass. "You're the man with the plan, Turk! You give the word and we sing the song."

The others voiced their agreement with the constantly moving Oboe, brandishing selected weapons and uttering threats of what they'd do after they'd located their evening's prey.

Throwing his massive gloved hands up, Turk demanded silence. As one they were quiet, and expectant looks turned upon the leering hood's face as he explained what he had in mind. When he was finished, he braced them with a fiendish stare, gently swaying his hips from side to side. "Any questions, you buncha pooper-poppers?"

There were none.

"Then let's do it, girls. Somewhere out there is tonight's entertainment. You just remember . . . if he's cute, *I* get to go first!"

Their bawdy laughter was swallowed up by a shrill clamor as a sudden brawl broke out between two teenage whores, their pimps gleefully placing bets on the winner while the hookers pummeled each other with clenched fists and painted nails.

The hunt was on.

"Can't eat another bite," groaned Calvin, pushing himself away from the table. Patting his disgustingly flat stomach, Bailey tilted his head back, exhaling a bloated sigh of contentment for Thornton's benefit.

They'd asked the cabbie to take them to the best seafood joint in town, and, much to their surprise, he'd done exactly that. Near the water, but far enough away from Fisherman's Wharf to remain reasonably priced, the restaurant offered the caliber of food San Francisco was known for worldwide.

Thornton, placing his fork on the white china plate, gratefully accepted a final cup of coffee from the hostess, who looked as if she'd stepped out of the pages of a fashion magazine. After she left, Bo sipped at the heavy ceramic captain's mug, the steaming coffee a perfect blend of two different South American beans.

Setting the cup down, he, too, pushed away from the table. "Whattaya say we walk a bit before heading back?"

Bailey nodded in agreement. "Good idea. I try to sleep on this tonight and it's nightmare city for sure. Wasn't there a park or something across the street?"

Thornton, craning his neck, looked past Bailey and through one of the huge plate-glass windows that made up the restaurant's front. Across the roadway he saw what appeared to be a miniature park, a narrow pathway leading into its lighted interior. "Looks that way from here. We can cut through it, maybe go a few blocks uphill, then flag a yellow down. It's not that late out."

Bailey, grabbing his cane, stood. "You buy, I'll fly,"

"Only if you tell me why the fuck you're carrying that piece of wood around. You screw yourself up since I last saw you?"

"Naww. It's just a little something I had a guy make for me. I'll tell you about it while we're working some of Davy Jones's Locker off."

Thornton laid his credit card on the table, signaling the hostess that they were through. "Don't forget the tip, asshole."

"That's what she said," responded Bailey when the woman leaned over the table, a bountiful supply of cleavage unburdening itself from her low-cut dress as the bill was collected.

"Let's go, squid. The only humpin' you're doing tonight is with me . . . on foot. Besides, that girl's not your type."

"Why's that?" asked Bailey.

Thornton waited until the shapely brunette had returned his card before answering the overfed SEAL. "She's pretty, polite, and obviously intelligent. Definitely not your type, no matter how you cut it."

"Fuck you," chuckled Calvin as they pushed through the door and into the night's salt-soaked air.

"Can't," retorted Thornton, "I forgot my rubbers in the cab."

Together they crossed the busy street, Bailey trying to smack Thornton on the shins with his cane, swearing profusely about his friend's lack of class.

Thornton knew they'd walked into an ambush. If asked, he couldn't say why, but he knew it. The air around him changed, the sounds from the street on either side of the small park suddenly diminished. He'd been here before, and he knew the drill.

He was about to say something to Bailey when three of them walked out of the trees, their chains jingling as they moved into position. Bo could tell they were carrying weapons, although he couldn't actually see what they were. Bailey nudged him as he heard the others cut them off from behind. "Back door's closed, my man. Looks like two more."

Both men waited where they stood.

Turk was pleased. They'd been hiding in the dark for nearly a half hour, waiting for the right opportunity to present itself. He'd elected to try the park by the wharf again. They'd scored big there several months ago. That time he and the boys found a college student and his girlfriend sitting on the steps of the tiny amphitheater that hosted street singers and mimes during the day. They'd surprised the young couple in the middle of a passionate kiss, robbing and raping the boy, then watching Oboe break the girls' kneecaps with a nunchaku.

It had been one of their better performances.

Now they'd scored on what looked like two dudes, one crippled and using a cane, the other obviously middle-aged. Seeing Oboe and Teddy-San slide in behind the pair of geeks, Turk decided to make this one quick. The meth was starting to peak, and he was anxious to get up to North Beach, where they could really party.

Thornton knew they'd have to fight. What pleased him was the ground the muggers had chosen for their attack. Although blocked from the front and rear, and boxed in by a thick hedge to their left, they still had access to the stage on their right flank. Whispering to Bailey that they needed to gain the stage, both men began to move slowly toward the platform's steps. No one spoke as both groups began to maneuver into position. Thornton wanted the high ground. The stage was built with a half-bowl over it, allowing access only from the front. If he and Bailey could position themselves so they could control their flanks and front, the battle would be half-won. If not, the goons would surround them, darting in and out until either Bailey or Thornton was downed. Then it would be like wolves in a pack, all on one and one on all.

"You can run, but *yoooou* can't hide," trilled Turk in a lilting falsetto. His comment was greeted by a round of laughter from the others.

"Fuck me to tears," grunted Bailey. "Look at 'em, Bo. They're all queers!"

"Big, mean queers, too," whispered Thornton. "Watch the tulip in the yellow shirt; he's the honcho. We get centered on the platform, go back to back. If they push it, kill 'em."

Bailey nodded. Gripping the cane tightly in his right hand, he began mounting the steps, taking each one at the same moment Thornton did. As they climbed the steps, he watched the band of leather-clad thugs break into a semicircle below them, their eyes glinting under the pale yellow light of the park's lamps.

"I want the cripple," intoned Oboe, twirling his chain-linked clubs in front of his body. "Cripples turn me on."

Turk laughed. "He's yours . . . but only after we fuck his buddy. Then he can watch while we play with his friend."

"Then we'll play with him again!" exclaimed one of the goons standing next to Turk. They all giggled, remembering the college kids they'd terrorized on this same spot.

"You guys must be bored to tears," quipped Bailey as he and Thornton reached center stage.

"Why's that, sweetlips!" This time it was the one called Teddy-San, who enjoyed dressing up like a Geisha girl in his spare time.

"It's pretty obvious, isn't it? I mean, look at you guys." Bailey paused, watching in amusement as they stared at each other in obedience to his suggestion. "You're all dressed up with no one to blow. . . ."

"Oh, shit!" muttered Thornton, and the fight was on.

Oboe leaped toward Bailey, the nunchaku making a sound like a high-speed buzz saw in the darkness. Dropping below the arc of the club, Bailey grasped the cane with both hands, then, coordinating the driving power of both his arms and legs, brought the end of the staff up between the screaming punk's legs. An autopsy would later show that the blow had been delivered with enough power to crack the subject's pelvic bone in two places.

Oboe lost the nunchaku, which bounced off the bowl's wall and skidded across the wooden flooring before coming to a stop. He felt his balls exploding—erupting really. Then it seemed that something gave way between his legs. Instinctively he grabbed the wooden cane with both hands. As his legs collapsed from beneath him, he rode the cane downward, his forehead nearly touching Bailey's hands, wrapped as they were around the now-trapped staff.

Calvin slid his hands back, feeling the hidden button and depressing it at the same time. Pulling rearward, he unsheathed the Hartsfield *wakizashi* from its artfully disguised scabbard, then, spinning the blade high above his head, he performed a perfect pirouette, bringing the gleaming edge down exactly where Oboe's head was joined to his neck.

Bailey was amazed at how easily the sword cut through the man's vertebrae.

As Oboe was making his attack on the "cripple," Turk ordered the two leather thugs alongside him to distract Thornton. The first man, spinning a bayonet in his hand, darted to Bo's left as his partner went to the right. Thornton held his ground until both men were nearly upon him, then rolled forward on his hands, somersaulting out from between the two. Coming up on his feet, he spun quickly and delivered a high snap kick directly into the chin of the bayonet wielder. His steel-toed boot shattered the man's jawbone, driving a mouthful of broken teeth down his throat. He dropped the knife where he stood, then turned to face Turk, whose eyes were staring at Oboe's decapitated body.

Policing up the bayonet, Bo sidestepped the second attacker, yelling at Bailey as he kicked the man squarely in the ass, propelling him toward the sword-swinging SEAL. Calvin was facing off with Teddy-San when Thornton's warning reached his ears. Shifting his stance so he could deliver a strike, should the assailant make a run at him, Bailey watched as the man flew past, arms flailing in a vain attempt to regain his balance.

Driving the butt of the sword's tang downward, Bailey grunted in satisfaction as it landed squarely above the man's unprotected kidney. When the organ exploded, searing pain overrode the screaming man's ability to control his bodily functions, a loathsome odor erupting from his grossly abused lower bowel.

Landing on his knees, the fatally damaged hood attempted to level his torso into an upright position, both hands pressed hard against his ruptured kidney, a silent howl hissing from between his bloodied lips.

Ignoring Teddy-San, who was spewing vomit over Oboe's head, Bailey stepped directly behind the injured man, raising the *waki* high above his head, then brought the whistling blade down with all the power he could muser. With a sound like a coconut being split with a hammer, the hard cranial bone parted, offering the off-white softness of the brain to his eager cutting edge. Calvin, his muscles swollen with adrenaline, continued the stroke, pulling the blade back toward himself as it roared through the sponge-like mass of brain cells, effortlessly parting the tough cartilege of the neck and throat, and continuing into the dead man's upper body.

Bailey's kendo instructor had told him of swords that could cut a man in half, but he'd never imagined he would witness, much less deliver, such an awesome blow. The blade finally stalled as it reached the upper abdomen, blood and mucus running freely down both sides of the hand-polished surface.

With a sharp kick, he freed the *waki*, then turned to face Teddy-San.

Thornton had only begun to witness Bailey's tremendous blow to the man's kidney when his attention was once again drawn to Turk. The man with no jaw now slumped to the stage, his life ebbing away while he slowly suffocated on his own teeth.

Turk was stunned. In less than a minute, three of his flunkies were dead or dying. Teddy-San was facing off with the crazy sword swinger, who was taunting him like a cat does a mouse. Oboe's eyes were staring at Turk, a frostlike glaze beginning to creep across them. The stink from Charlie O's splintered carcass hung over the killing ground like a thick fog, its aroma a noxious mixture of blood, shit, urine, and body gases. Turk wanted to run, to hide, to shrink from the eyes of the huge motherfucker only steps away from him.

Turk believed in hell, and now one of its demons was facing him, expressionless, unmoving, deadly. He pulled the combat tomahawk from where it hung suspended behind his neck, and with a fury born of terror, charged hell's own praetorian.

Teddy-San burped out the last of his stomach's fill, wiping a sticky hand across his rouged lips. In the other he held a long-bladed Magnum tanto, its blade stained with his sweat and puke. His eyes locked onto the madman's in front of him. It never occured to him to run, to flee like a frightened deer down the steps and into the safety of the park's thick woods. Dope did that to a man. It fucked up the senses, confused the instincts, rendered him oblivious to the obvious.

Because, obviously, Teddy was going to die.

"You're history, fag-buddy. History. You might as well bend over and spread 'em, because once I jam this beauty up your ass, it'll all be over except the cryin'." Bailey could hear Thornton locking it up with the gang's leader, their grunts and lurid invectives exploding behind him as he pushed toward his own opponent.

Finally, Teddy-San could stand the patient stalking no longer. Rushing low, hoping to escape the lethal blade's hungry edge through speed and agility, Teddy quickly closed the gap between himself and Bailey. Seeing an opening, he ripped upward with the tanto, only to have Calvin's spinning form evaporate in front of him.

Calvin pulled the sword back at chest level, then drove it hard into the mystified punk's exposed side. The *waki* neatly skewered the man from side to side, exploding his heart, piercing his lungs, killing him before the tanto could finish bouncing off the hard oaken flooring of the stage.

Slipping the dripping sword from Teddy's leather-bound corpse, the exhausted narc turned to witness Turk's final moments on earth.

The massive hardcase hurled himself at Thornton, a war cry escaping from hs wide-open mouth, the tomahawk gripped tightly in both hands. Rather than meet the charge head on, Bo dropped back, throwing the captured bayonet at Turk's face.

The hard plastic handle struck the rampaging man's forehead, splitting it so that a quick rush of bright red blood cascaded into his eyes, slowing him enough so Thornton could sidestep the assault. Snarling in victory, the veteran of more firefights than he cared to remember whipped the ear-popping stiletto free of its sheath, using his other arm to trap the disoriented man's head in a viselike grip that Satan himself couldn't break.

Slipping his right foot behind Turk's left knee, Thornton kicked hard until the man dropped to the ground. Unwilling to release the struggling leather attacker, Thornton watched as the man began wildly swinging the razor-sharp tomahawk, his target the big commando's exposed throat. Just as it appeared a blow would connect, Thornton felt a rush of cool air sweep past his face, then heard the dull *thunk* of Bailey's blade as it separated Turk's hatchet-wielding hand from his wrist.

Throwing his body weight to one side, Bo twisted the gasping thug's head sideways so that he could clearly see every hair that was growing out of Turk's ear canal. Positioning the knife directly over the ear, Thornton momentarily remembered the old Cuban's advice to push it hard into the opening so that the needlelike point would burst into the brain, killing immediately.

With a sharp exhalation, Thornton dropped his full weight behind the thrust. He felt Turk's body go rigid, heard the momentary beating of the pointed boots against the platform's surface, then smelled the ball of pent-up air that escaped from the dead man's lungs as he went limp in Bo's grip.

Forcing himself up, Thornton made eye contact with Bailey. Receiving a thumbs-up from the blood-spattered SEAL, Bo stooped to retrieve the bayonet which held his fingerprints prisoner. Both men dropped from the platform, moving quickly into the shadows.

Somewhere out on the bay, a foghorn sounded, warning those at sea to take care as they crossed under the broad span of the Gate's massive arch.

CHAPTER

6

"Your breakfast, sir." Lippman, looking up from his freshly printed *San Francisco Chronicle*, nodded to the waiter, who expertly slid a heaping plate of eggs, sausage, and toast onto the table. "Will that be all for now?"

"Yes, thank you." Thinking to remind the waiter he would be joined by two guests, Lippman indicated he'd appreciate the same prompt service when they arrived. The man nodded, slipping the five-dollar bill Lippman offered into his breast pocket.

Lippman was seated so that his table commanded a view of the dining room's entranceway while still remaining semisecluded. Buttering a thick slice of whole-wheat toast, he pondered whether or not Thornton would agree to watchdog Montalvo after yesterday's meeting. Should he decline, the FBI team could *probably* stay in place, although Lippman wanted a second unit brought in as backup. State's file on Aguilar's security branch was implicit in its description of the colonel's elite group of paramilitary assassins. They were mature, blooded, and exceptionally adept at planning their operations, an attribute Lippman credited to their months of training with the Israelis in both Tel Aviv and Lebanon.

If Aguilar put his hounds on Montalvo's scent, the odds were in their favor.

Burrowing into his food, Lippman switched his train of thought to Bailey and Thornton. After they'd left, he'd contacted his office in D.C. and requested a computer scan of both men. Milk, as usual, was quick to get back to him. Regrettably, the results were mixed.

Bailey was the easier of the two. The computer revealed his military record as a Navy SEAL, his tours of duty in Latin America and elsewhere, and his honorable discharge. It showed him currently assigned to the DEA office in Washington, under the supervision of a station chief named Billings. His record with the DEA was as impressive as his service with the Navy had been, and he appeared to be an up-and-comer within the agency.

Thornton, however, was a different story. Milk's attempt to access the man's file was denied by the computer. Adding to that frustration was the fact that Lippman's access code number had been recorded and forwarded to something called Annex IV at the NSA. Milk had been frantic about the forwarding, explaining to Lippman that it was a security procedure reserved strictly for presidentially sanctioned projects. No doubt they'd be receiving a visit from some spook in the NSA about their interest in Thornton, an interest Milk wondered if they could justify.

Calming his assistant as best as he could over a phone, Lippman considered the effort worthwhile. He'd have to call State and ask them to run interference on the computer probe, but the secretary would see the NSA was pacified, even if he had to take the matter directly to Bush. More important, Lippman now possessed confirmation that Thornton was a sanctioned agent, an agent with direct access to the Oval Office. Annex IV was a bonus, no doubt a covert link within the NSA which handled Thornton. Bailey was probably nothing more than a convenient gopher, his military background and positioning with the DEA making him acceptable to Thornton as an intermediary for meetings like yesterday's.

Knowledge was power, reflected Lippman between bites. And power was to be used in appropriate measures toward the accomplishment of a desired goal. Lippman's goal was Montalvo's value to the United States. Whether the Latin politician went on to become his country's next president or faced a firing squad personally commanded by Aguilar was of little consequence to the man from State. What he cared about was keeping the subject alive and happy long enough for his fate to be decided by powers greater than either him or Montalvo. Knowing as much about Thornton as possible would help him accomplish his goal.

He spotted the two men entering the dining room a split second before they recognized him. As they crossed the room to his

table, Lippman sensed a difference in their attitudes from yesterday. They were like huge cats on the prowl, each movement
precise, every action taking place around them noted. Lippman
had seen the same kind of behavior in the secret war zones of
Angola, Chad, Nicaragua, and Guatemala. The men now pulling
out chairs at his table were predators. Intelligent, well-trained,
battle-proven artists in the craft of deliberate mayhem.

He wished he'd waited for them to arrive before eating, the
food in his stomach becoming a sodden lump as Bailey and
Thornton seated themselves, two cobras a hair's breadth away
from striking.

Without preamble, Thornton spoke. His voice was low, like
distant thunder, each word distinct, every inflection rich with
intent. "I want to meet with Montalvo. Now. Alone. You'll have
your answer immediately afterward."

Lippman forced a half-chewed chunk of slightly greasy sausage down his throat. Trying to buy time so he could counterat-
tack Thornton's bull-like charge, he said what he knew would be
expected from him. "It can be arranged. But not at the drop of a
hat. I'll have to contact the FBI agent in charge, clear the meeting
with Montalvo, arrange for a cover unit—"

Thornton, with an abrupt wave of his callused hand, cut him
off at the ankles. "Bullshit. Bailey and I know Montalvo's in this
hotel, probably in the Presidential Suite seeing how State likes to
spread the taxpayers' wealth around. Just finish your fucking
breakfast and let's do it . . . or me and my friend here will *adios*
on out the door."

The artery responsible for moving oxygen-rich blood to Lippman's brain began throbbing as his anger at being talked to like
an office boy overwhelmed his attempts at diplomacy. How dare
this glorified thug treat him like a three-eared mule! Fuck Annex
IV! Fuck the DEA's overmuscled escort service! And most of all,
fuck this *Mr.* Thornton . . . a man whose first name he apparently
didn't rate knowing.

Lippman was about to blast them right out of their seats when
Bailey took the wind from his sails.

"We killed five people last night, Mr. Lippman. Five nasty
cocksuckers who wanted to kick our butts just because we were
there. Neither of us is in the mood to play patty-cake with you

about meeting with my man Ricky. You may not like the hand, but it's not up to you whether you play it or fold. I suggest you reach down between your legs, grab yourself by the sack, and start putting it together. Because something tells me if you blow this one, King George may send you to some Fourth World capital for the duration of your career. . . ."

Lippman sagged at the grim-faced agent's words. He'd read about the five alleged homosexuals being slaughtered in some beachside park the night before. The reporter writing the story mentioned that all five were linked by police to earlier assaults and rapes in the San Francisco area. The gay community had released a statement condemning the sad state of law enforcement, avoiding reference to the sexual preferences of the dead men.

In a whisper, Lippman asked if they'd left anything the police could use to link them to the scene.

"Nothing," spat Bailey. "I called my people this morning. They've already alerted the local office as to the 'problem.' Should anything come up that would point the cops toward us, DEA'll take over the case as an ongoing drug investigation, and that'll be the end of it."

Lippman sighed. Taking Bailey's analogy to heart, he decided to fold rather than play the hand dealt him. At least he'd still be in the game. "I take it you don't want anything to eat before meeting Montalvo?"

Thornton flashed Bailey a wide grin, then turned to Lippman. "Actually we're both pretty hungry, now that you mention it. How about ordering us what you had, we'll chow down while you're muzzling the local FBI. Meet you upstairs in, say, an hour?"

Lippman nodded. After ordering for the two commandos, he started for the elevator, wondering how Thornton and Bailey could eat after killing five people in the manner the paper had so graphically described. Watching the twin doors of the lift close to form a steel barrier between himself and the outside world, Lippman then began worrying how the two men knew of Montalvo's location. If Thornton and Bailey could figure it out, he ruminated, couldn't Aguilar's henchmen, too?

CHAPTER

7

Ricardo Montalvo watched as Lippman left the room. He was both amused and perplexed at the State Department official's mood, best described as being one of high anxiety. So Lippman wanted him to meet privately with this Señor Thornton? What of it? Montalvo had been meeting all sorts of odd government characters since his arrival in San Francisco, what was one more faceless name?

It wasn't as if he had plans for the day.

Montalvo walked across the plush carpet of his suite's conference room, peeking momentarily through the curtained bay window overlooking the eastern section of the city. He was of medium height and build, with aristocratic features, although he knew of no such blood in his family. His coal black hair was thick, and freshly cut by the Fairmont's in-house barber. A robust moustache enhanced his subtle masculinity, although it was Montalvo's eyes that were his strongest asset. They were a startling shade of blue, capable of being as encouraging as a warm summer day, or as bitter as an Alaskan glacier. He recognized the effect his eyes had on people, and he was gifted in how he used them.

On this particular morning, he wore a pair of elephant gray wool slacks, black leather loafers, and a black polo shirt that lacked any particular designer's emblem. Secured to his wrist was a new Seiko, replacing the one taken by Melendez's bandits. He hadn't had the money or time to replace their wedding rings.

Allowing the curtain to fall, Montalvo turned as the door opened, the FBI agent known as Curt tossing him a quick smile.

The man Lippman told him about stepped quickly into the room, his eyes taking everything in at once. Without speaking, he motioned for the door to be closed, waiting until they'd both heard the soft click of the latch falling into·place before stepping forward. Montalvo observed him patiently, hands clasped together behind his back, an expression of expectation on his face.

"Señor Montalvo, please allow me the courtesy of introducing myself. My name is Beaumont Thornton. I have been asked to perform a service for you and your family, but first I must satisfy myself that the potential risk is worth the possible sacrifice. For that reason I have asked for only moments of your time."

Montalvo smiled. "You speak my language very well, Mr. Thornton."

"As you do mine, sir." Thornton waited only a moment before shaking Montalvo's outstretched hand. He approved of the man's firm grip, responding with one of his own.

"Please sit. We can speak English if you wish, I enjoy the practice."

Both men ignored the table and heavy wooden chairs provided for them. Instead, they chose to sit at a small couch near the double glass doors leading onto a small balcony. Thornton noted that the doors were bolted, although the heavy cream-colored drapes were open. There were no buildings of equal or greater height opposite the balcony's view.

"You have eaten?" asked Montalvo.

"Yes, thank you." Looking around, Thornton wondered if the room were bugged. Remembering Lippman's reputation, he decided it was. "I would like you to relate the details of your escape to me, briefly, as I know you have done this before. I am especially interested in the day you and your family were to have been executed."

Montalvo leaned back, a quiet puff of air coming from his lips. Fixing Thornton with a tolerant eye, he related the story without pause or emotion.

". . . and that is how the Montalvos came to be in this beautiful city, Mr. Thornton. It is not a charming story, I admit. But it is the truth, and hopefully that is what you wanted to hear."

Bo nodded his head. Whether the gesture was meant in agreement to his last statement or in appreciation for the story he had heard, Montalvo wasn't sure. He understood why Lippman was unsettled by the intense man sitting before him. Men of Thornton's breed had bad effects on snakes like Lippman.

Thornton broke their silence. "What would you do if the United States elects to return you to La Libertad?"

Montalvo, his hands held open in frankness, answered the question he thought about every waking moment. "I would die, of course. Aguilar has no choice but to make me what he claims I am. It is an easy question, Mr. Thornton."

"If you are elected, what will become of Aguilar and people like Melendez?" Thornton recognized the spark of fury that burst into flames as Montalvo digested the question. He listened closely to the man's response, attempting to "feel" the answer more than hear it.

"The man in me would want to avenge the dead whose bodies were blown to bits as I saved my family and myself. He would delight in cutting the balls from between Aguilar's shaking legs, then feeding them one by one to his dogs. The man in me wants nothing more than to drop the *putas* like Melendez from an army helicopter, and watch them splatter against the sharp lava the same way so many of the disappeared did. *That* is what the man in me wants to do.

"But I could not allow that part of my being to wreak such a terrible havoc against these animals, as much as they deserve it. To do so would betray my soul. It would show me to be no better than they are, perhaps worse.

"If the people of my country decide that I am worthy of their trust, I will bring the criminals to justice under the laws we have always guided ourselves by. If they flee, we shall seek them out. If they beg for mercy, we shall listen. If they repent, we will forgive. But they will pay a just price for the crimes they have committed, that I can promise you!"

Thornton was impressed. Try as he might, he couldn't find a hole in the man's story, or deceit in his convictions. It might be worth a shot, he thought to himself. At least they could give Montalvo a fighting chance while State made up its mind.

"Señor Thornton?" Montalvo was speaking again, his face reflecting a quizzical smile. "You know much about me, yet I know little of you."

Thornton nodded his acknowledgment of the man's statement. "I'm afraid I can't enlighten you to the extent you have me, sir," he replied. "What has Lippman told you?"

"Señor Lippman only said that you were a 'security expert.' Why, I asked him, do I need a security expert when I am surrounded by the FBI?"

Both men laughed.

"Señor Montalvo, in a sense Lippman is correct. I command a team of specialists, men who have been in this business for a long time. Lippman is concerned that Aguilar may send his people after you and your family, that current precautions may not be enough. He wants my people here until State decides your case."

Montalvo nodded his understanding. "Lippman is astute. Aguilar cannot let me live. If your State Department returns us to La Libertad, there will be no problem. If not, he will try to liquidate us within your borders. He knows he will be ousted in the elections, then where will he go? Perhaps Panama? Noriega is his brother when it comes to sucking at the Devil's tit."

Both men were silent, content for the moment with their own thoughts. To an observer they appeared as old friends, respectful of each other's privacy, content to wait until the other was ready to continue the conversation.

"These people, they are your friends?" Montalvo asked.

"Yes," Thornton replied, "they are my friends as well as my people."

"That explains why you are so careful before making a commitment. You are a soldier, no?"

Bo stood, pouring himself a glass of iced water from the pitcher provided. "I *was* a soldier. Now I work for myself."

Montalvo looked at his watch, then moved so he stood opposite the former Snake-Eater. "If you accept this 'job,' would you be our protectors? Or our jailers?"

Finishing his water, Thornton placed the glass gently on the table, then turned to face Montalvo, who was studying him in frank anticipation. "*Señor*, are the two not one in the same?"

Montalvo clapped his hands together in appreciation. "You are wise, *amigo*. I trust you and your friends are as good as Lippman seems to believe. The colonel's dogs are determined, and they are well trained. You will not be facing the level of scum we suffered under on the killing grounds. These will be young professionals, schooled in the art of killing by many knowledgeable governments . . . to include your own."

"Do you know if Melendez lived through the attack?" asked Thornton. "It's important because Aguilar may send him to finish the job he failed at. It would give us someone to look for, a face we would recognize in a crowd."

Thornton could see the agony of the memory etching its way into the Latin's features. His eyes clouded as he looked beyond Thornton. He was once again running from the gunfire, cursing his wife's stumbling, urging his daughter forward. The screams of the dying and frightened rose above the whine of the bullets, an unholy tenor chasing Montalvo as he struggled up the arroyo. It was only then he remembered the lone guardsman who stepped from nowhere into their path, a pistol in his hand, blood seeping from the cuts on his brutal face. Montalvo recalled the man lurching for Maritza, her shriek of pure horror at his touch. Pushing his wife out of the line of fire, Montalvo found himself staring down the massive hole of the soldier's .45. Without thinking, he had swung the captured assault rifle's barrel on target, firing a long burst from the hip. . . .

"Señor Montalvo? Ricardo? Are you all right?" It was Thornton, alarmed at the flashes of pain, hate, and satisfaction that were arcing through Montalvo's cobalt blue eyes.

"*Sì, sì, estoy bien.* I am fine," he said. "Forgive me, Thornton. I remembered killing a man, a soldier of Aguilar's. He was deep in the arroyo, alone. He touched my daughter, and I killed him."

"Probably part of a listening post or roadblock party. Must have escaped from the G's, then stumbled into you by accident." Bo looked closely at the man in front of him. "First man you've ever killed?"

Ricardo Montalvo nodded.

Thornton took the man by both shoulders, shaking him gently, challenging the smoldering eyes. "Fuck him, Ricardo. He would have killed you, your wife, ultimately your daughter. He wasn't a soldier, he was a savage. He deserved to die."

"Thank you, Thornton. Coming from you, I can believe that."

Thornton smiled, pleased he had gotten through to the man.

"Hey, call me Bo; all my friends do," he said as he released his grip on Montalvo.

Montalvo in turn grasped the commando hard about his corded arms. "Does Dick Lips call you that?" he whispered in a conspiratorial tone.

Thornton erupted in laughter at the mention of Lippman's nickname. "Fuck me, no!" he exclaimed. "Lippman calls me mister . . . and always better, or I'll kick his bureaucratic ass."

Lippman's face gushed dark crimson at the laughter that exploded inside his head. Removing the headphones, he managed to hold his anger in check, telling himself that at least the two men were hitting it off. That would bring Thornton and his team in, and none too soon. Milk's early-morning report was a bombshell. If they did it the way the secretary wanted, Mr. Damn-You-to-Hell Thornton was going to have his work cut out for him.

But Lippman would let the bastard commit himself before sharing the news. A satisfied smirk fragmented his face as the door to the conference room opened.

CHAPTER

8

"Whose bullshit idea was *this*?" barked Jason Silver, pushing his glasses back on his nose. The ex-Ranger sat on a sofa in the DEA safe house's living room, a Moeller throwing knife balanced in his hand, the broad-tipped blade snapping and popping in the light as he moved it from side to side.

The rest of the team's eyes turned to Thornton, who'd finished explaining what would be expected of them. Lippman's assessment of the Springblade leader had been only semi-correct, Thornton indeed was pissed, but not enough to walk out the door after telling Montalvo he could count on the team covering them. "Only the State Department could fuck up a wet dream this badly," he'd told Lippman, "but if we don't grab the bear by the ears, you cum bubbles will end up getting a shitload of people waxed for nothing. My people will be here in twenty-four hours."

Bailey and he made the calls. Hartung flew in first, as he only needed to catch a hop from San Diego. The sergeant major was Thornton's business partner in a dive shop they co-owned, and a legend in the special-operations community. Thirty years of kicking ass the world over made him an invaluable presence on the team; it had been his finger that sent Tony Dancer down in flames when Springblade smoked his mountain retreat.

Bo's call to Linda resulted in the girl driving up to Seaside, where Jason Silver now made his home. Silver, a former Ranger with two tours in Vietnam, was Thornton's right-hand man. He was the team's top gun when it came to things that went *bang* in the night, and a commo wizard whose skills were second only to Hartung's. Linda found the diminutive night stalker immersed in his latest hobby, his backyard studded with a series of plywood targets whose fronts were embedded with expensive throwing knives from Harald Moeller and Harry McEvoy. It took him only an hour to pack.

The news on David Lee was disappointing. Lee was the team's only active-duty operative. A stone-cold expert in light and heavy weapons, Sergeant First Class Lee could dead-center an eighty-one mike-mike through a Hula Hoop, or center-punch a man's face at fifteen hundred meters with a McMillian .50. Fully recovered from wounds received during their breakout from Alpine, Lee returned to the 7th Special Forces Group at Fort Bragg. From there he was attached to the battalion in Panama.

Bailey's call to SOCOM confirmed what he and Thornton had gotten from Rumor Control, Lee and his team were currently operational. That meant they'd gone "over the wire" for the SOUTHCOM commander.

That left Thornton short one man. Bo wanted a man on each of the Montalvos, especially since Lippman's briefing about the concept of the operation. In addition, he needed a relief man, someone to spell them when they got tired, or were needed elsewhere. He'd requested a replacement for Lee, and Bailey found him one.

"Everyone knows Dave's op-conned," Thornton told the expectant group, "we sure as hell hope his team has a successful mission. . . ."

"Airborne and amen!" interrupted Hartung.

"In the meantime," Bo continued, "we'll be taking on a straphanger who, Calvin says, is worth a shit. I'll let him make the introductions, since Bannion is one of his children."

Bailey stepped forward, motioning to the man at his side that it was time to meet the team. Mike Bannion stood up from the chair he'd taken when the meeting began. He was of average height, his frame heavily packed with muscle from hours of weight lifting and exercise. His face appeared to have been laser-cut from spring steel, long brown hair touching his aircraft-carrier shoulders. With emerald green eyes that lit up whenever he smiled or laughed, Bannion was considered good-natured by those he worked with.

Those whom he worked against considered him hellish, but then, most of them were dead.

"This is Mike Bannion. He's detached from one of our special units until this gig is over. Mike served with the SEALs, like me"—hoots, boos, and hisses erupting from Silver and Hartung —"but he earned most of his hazardous-duty pay in the Middle East." Bailey flipped the two hecklers the bird, then continued. "Mike speaks Spanish, courtesy of DLI, and is a weapons man, like Lee. He was both mine and Billings's first choice when we made our request, and he'll be there when you need him. Mike?"

Bannion looked up from the floor, where he'd been keeping his eyes during Bailey's introduction. He hated times like this; it embarrassed him, although he didn't know why. Being center stage was never to his liking, one of the reasons he fit so well into the kind of operations SLAM conducted. No heroes, no stars, just results generated by team effort.

"If you know Calvin Bailey," he began, "you know he's fulla shit." The room convulsed in appreciative laughter, Bailey taking a couple hard shots to the shoulder from Silver. Becoming serious, the SLAM agent continued, knowing that no matter what his background or current status, he was the new kid on the block. This was a hard-core team, that he could tell. They might accept him up front, but he'd have to prove his mettle starting now. That was the way it was in the Forces.

"I don't know anything about this mission, or about your team. Twenty-four hours ago I got the word, and I grabbed the first thing smokin' for the West Coast.

"Cal mentioned SLAM. It's obvious that the security clearances in this room are so high you could all be busted"—another burst of laughter, the pleasant sound encouraging Bannion—"so I feel comfortable telling you that I'm what our circle calls a 'SLAM dunker.'

"What that means is that I do what Bailey says you all did to Tony Dancer's organization. My team is based outta Colombia, but we go anywhere, anytime, and do anything that's necessary. I did some shit with the Navy, like Cal, but that was long ago and far away. My specialty is weapons, urban combat, executive and diplomatic protection. I'm no hero, but I am a Seahawks fan."

After Bannion finished, Thornton took the floor. He was

pleased with the reception Mike received from the team. Bo was comfortable with Bailey's recommendation—hell, that's how he'd made some of the teams he'd been on. Special Forces owned the rights to the "Old Boy Network." Once you earned the hat, the clock started on your reputation within the organization. Your assignments, schools, missions, friends, social behavior, successes, and fuckups were all recorded by someone, some- where. Most of the time it was by the team sergeants. A man could be made or broken by a team daddy's recommendation, although that wasn't always the case. The SEALs, Force Recon, CCT, DELTA, and any other elite military organization operated in much the same way. Information was shared when necessary, reputations confirmed, recommendations made.

"Okay, let's get started. I'm happy Mike's on board; make him comfortable and maybe he'll stay. We've got zero time on this one, since State threw us a curve ball. Listen close, if you need clarification, ask.

"State's stooge is a guy named Lippman. He's a buddy-fucker, so watch out. He does *not* have operational control once we're in place. He will be on observer status for the duration, and if the Montalvos go east, or back down south, he'll be their escort.

"State is having problems confirming Ricardo Montalvo's story. Aguilar is covering his tracks pretty well, and State's hav- ing to go through their intel sources at the embassy in La Liber- tad. It's my understanding that the MilGrp down there has cultivated some insiders who are close to the colonel, and they will probably give up the necessary information.

"In the meantime, State is *officially* going to agree to turn Montalvo and family over to a representative from Aguilar's em- bassy here in San Francisco"—Bo noted the raised eyebrows, although no one spoke—"but here's where it gets weird.

"There's an exiled priest named Delgado who runs a church here in the city. He's on Aguilar's hit list, too, and is an outspo- ken critic of the regime. . . ."

Hartung's gruff voice rumbled across the room. "Isn't he the one who was on *60 Minutes* a month or so ago? Heads up a sanctuary movement for political refugees or something."

"One and the same, Sergeant Major. Delgado provides a safe haven on church grounds for people fleeing La Libertad and other

Central or South American dictatorships. He's a personal friend of Montalvo's, and agreed to give the family sanctuary until State clears Ricardo's name."

Silver jumped from the sofa, grabbing a sandwich off a nearby table. "So why doesn't this Lippman have one of State's limos run the family downtown to Delgado's?"

Thornton pulled up a chair and sat. "The reason is, that State's been playing both sides. They can't jump off Aguilar's bus because the G's now happen to control the entire eastern half of La Libertad—the colonel would go nuts and we'd lose the country for sure.

"On the other hand, if State can stall long enough for the elections to be held, Montalvo will beat the colonel hands down. So everyone's on a tightrope until State blesses Montalvo, thereby creating a basis for denying Aguilar's request for extradition, thereby making it possible to keep the man in the U.S. until the elections take place."

"Fuck me to tears, Bo. That was *beautiful*! You sound just as screwed up as Lippman."

"Button it, squid," growled Hartung. "The man's making sense for the first time since I met him. Don't fuck it up by interrupting."

Thornton smiled. He realized how much he'd missed them since they'd parted company several months before. Scanning the room, he studied each and every face, knowing he was once again among friends . . . and warriors.

"So where's the shit in the laundry, Bo?"

"I'm glad you asked, Mike. State can't deliver Montalvo to Delgado; that would blow the whole thing, and Aguilar would cry 'foul' to the United Nations, who in turn would demand that the order for extradition be enforced.

"What Lippman wants us to do is break the Montalvos out of State's custody, and move them to the church. Once we've got them there, Delgado will extend sanctuary and tell the media monsters that an unidentified terrorist group engineered the breakout, and that the Montalvos then ran from them . . . making their way to Delgado's and asking for asylum because they don't know who to trust any longer."

Silver's throwing knife whipped over their heads, neatly burying itself deep within the papered wall. "Well, shit, this is more complicated than an episode of *Murder, She Wrote*. We're supposed to rip off the FB-fucking-I, deliver the family to some crazy priest who Aguilar wants dead, too, then hang around and play guardian angel until State washes its hands of one shitbird so they can pick up another.

"I love it. I really fucking love it. Nothing's changed since the Nam, has it? I mean, we *still* don't know what we're doing, or we haven't the balls to say *no* to the bad guys while giving the good dudes whatever they need to kick ass and take names."

Hartung, pulling the twelve-and-a-half-inch knife from the wall, turned to Bailey and waited until Silver finished speaking. "Who's paying the bills on this dump?" he asked.

"State," replied Bailey with a grin.

"Fuck it then; it needs repainting, anyway." The sun-bronzed veteran of Korea, Vietnam, and a few wars in between, spun the highly polished blade so it sat handle first in his thick palm, then, in a flash of blurred movement, he entombed the knife between Silver's polished jungle boots. "Watch where you throw that thing, Junior. Next time I'll stick it where the sun don't shine. *Comprendez vous?*"

"Damn, Sergeant Major!" Jason exclaimed. "I didn't know you could throw a knife! Maybe we can practice together, huh? Shit, I bet you used to throw fucking knives with Moses while he was killin' time between cross-border ops into the Promised Land."

Hartung threw a scowl at the grinning man. "You demo guys are all alike," he sputtered, "crazy as loons and dumb as dirt!"

Thornton regained control of the meeting. They were professionals, and he knew they'd heard everything he said, but there wasn't any time for fooling around. "Listen up!" he yelled over the din Silver and the sergeant major were creating. Getting their attention, he pointed at Bailey. "What's the word on funding?"

Calvin, his cane resting across both knees, answered. "State agrees to your fee. Half the money was wired to the account numbers you gave as soon as each man checked in from the airport. The rest will be paid on completion of the mission. Insurance and expenses are covered one hundred percent.

"Weapons and any other equipment we might need will be

provided by our office here. The Army has a Special Forces unit headquartered in San Francisco, so any high-speed/low-drag stuff can come from them.

"Billings sends his best . . . says he'll be pushing State's investigation from his end. In the meantime, we're supposed to snatch Montalvo no later than tomorrow night. Lippman's supposed to turn them over to Aguilar's goons the day after, and if they ain't gone . . . they will be, dig?"

They all "dug." Springblade needed to move quickly, or Ricardo Montalvo would find himself, his wife, and his beautiful daughter in another cage before the week was out.

CHAPTER

▬▬▬▬▬

9

Hartung dropped them off a half-block from the hotel. Giving Thornton a slight nod, the sergeant major slipped the turbo automatic into drive, quickly pulling back into the evening's traffic. They waited until his taillights became lost, then headed toward the Fairmont. The three men blended easily into the city's nightly crush. Within minutes they reached the hotel, taking a moment before crossing the crowded street to pull a visual recon.

"There's Lippman," pointed out Silver. Indeed, the man from State was already entering the lobby of San Francisco's most elegant lodging.

"He's right on schedule," commented Thornton, "should hang around the desk for a minute or two after calling up to Montalvo's room, then be on his way to the elevator."

With the light in their favor, the men quickly crossed the busy intersection, Thornton and Bannion continuing down to a lower-level entrance as Silver sauntered in the way Lippman had chosen. Without glancing around, the pugnacious demo man made his way to where Lippman stood, a bank of elevators pumping like pistons to service the hotel's guests. Touching the policeman's sap in his pocket, Silver allowed himself a small smile. He was really going to enjoy this.

Both men took an involuntary step backward as the door slid open with a quiet hiss. A tall blond, her sensual figure sheathed in a black velvet dress, casually stepped out of the elevator's interior. Silver stared appreciatively as she floated by, a scent like that of spring flowers trailing behind her. The dress she wore left his imagination a smoldering hulk, its fit outlining every crease and curve of her well-tuned frame. Following Lippman into the now empty-compartment, he silently applauded the city's gay community. The more of them around, he reasoned, the more women like *that* would be available for guys like him.

Silver shuffled over to a corner away from Lippman, then turned and fixed his eyes above the elevator's door, assuming the standard appearance of a bored elevator passenger. While Lippman inserted a key giving him access to the penthouse's floor, Silver leaned forward and depressed one of the softly glowing buttons on the control panel.

No one else joined them.

Silver watched as the doors slid closed. He could still smell the woman's fragrance, teasingly lingering in the elevator's cramped space. Even as thick cables whisked them toward their destinations, Silver ignored the curious glance Lippman gave him, then, as the man looked away, slipped the heavy sap from his pocket and swung it against Lippman's exposed head.

The blow made a sharp slapping sound when it connected, the force of impact driving Lippman sideways into the wall. Silver remained in a crouch in case his man was down but not out. Lippman didn't move.

A soft bell-like noise alerted Silver they were about to reach the floor whose button he'd pushed. Storing the sap, he delivered a kick to Lippman's exposed groin, smiling in satisfaction at the unconscious man's grunt when it connected. Bo told them to make it look good. Besides, from everything he'd heard about Lippman, the man deserved a good quick kick in the balls.

The elevator stopped, gave a little hop as the cables adjusted themselves, then the doors rolled back to reveal Bannion and Thornton. The men had taken a set of fire stairs to the second floor, then waited for Silver to arrive. Bannion had driven an elderly couple off who'd joined them seconds earlier, his fart so noxious even Thornton was appalled at its ferocity.

"He's out cold," smirked Silver. "The key's in the lock, just turn and push override, we'll be upstairs in no time."

Thornton glanced at the collapsed form, noting the thin trickle of spittle running down one corner of Lippman's open mouth. "How hard you hit him?" he asked Silver.

"A love tap, Bo. I swear it on my mother's grave. He just *looks* like the shit was beat outta him."

Bannion watched as Thornton turned the key, then punched the elevator's red override button so they would go directly to the penthouse without stopping. Reaching into the pocket of his black satin jacket, Mike withdrew a seven-inch suppressor and began screwing the dull black extension onto the threaded portion of his Colt .45's barrel. Bannion would be the only one actually doing any shooting, his magazines carrying loaded-down rounds which were powerful enough to cycle the action of his pistol, but incapable of seriously hurting anyone hit by them. The FBI team on duty were warned to wear their vests, and if they followed orders, the worst they could expect would be some convincing bruises.

Turning to Thornton, Bannion wagged the fully assembled pistol back and forth, indicating to the big commando leader they were ready for phase two. Silver's job was to dump Lippman in the Montalvo apartment, and afterward to man the elevator while his companions effected the family's breakout. Thornton's arrangements earlier that day included telling the elder Montalvo to take his family to the conference room so they could be found easily. At the same time, Bo didn't want the women to witness the staged performance, knowing it could reopen barely scabbed-over memories of El Refugio.

Again the elevator hopped to a stop.

"Make it look good, Mike. The FBI boys are going to take a lot of heat for losing these people, so let's give them enough to convince the cameras they're lucky to be alive."

"Roger that, Bo. One rock 'em—sock 'em Clint Eastwood special coming up!"

Checking Lippman, who hadn't moved yet, Thornton again asked Silver how hard he'd zapped the man. Jason's face glowed with mock indignation as he answered. "I'm tellin' you, Bo, it was an angel's kiss. This sissy-la-la just has a soft noggin; he'll be fine in an hour or two."

Thornton nodded, stepping into the hallway with Bannion. Both men pulled red Nomex hoods over their heads, followed by gloves of the same color. The hallway was quiet, as empty as the Savior's tomb. With a flick of his finger, Thornton identified their direction of travel. Bannon dog-trotted down the corridor, with Thornton close behind. Bo felt the weight of his cocked and locked 645 beneath the light Windbreaker he was wearing. Both Silver and he were packing, but unlike Bannion's, their rounds were full-bore body breakers. One never knew who might have the same idea in mind.

Reaching the ornately carved oak door, both men assumed standard door-busting positions. Bannion locked eyes with Thornton, who nodded in anticipation. With a quick series of raps against the oiled finish, the SLAM dunk artist beckoned the apartment's occupants to answer.

"Maybe that's them?" The speaker was a heavyset agent named Foster.

"Want to answer it, or you want me to?"

Foster heaved himself out of the leather chair he'd been sitting in for over an hour. "Naw, Curt, I'll do it. Might as well get this over with. Besides," he laughed, "who knows how bad these guys will fuck you and Marty up? I might get over, being first in line."

Curt shook his head at the senior agent's comment. "I don't like this. Just doesn't seem right, us getting our asses kicked on purpose and all."

Foster adjusted the bullet-resistant vest so that it covered his chest and stomach. Tucking his shirt back into his pants, he tugged his suit coat on, feeling the empty holster at his side. They'd been told to leave their guns on the table, unloaded, so that no one would react by sheer instinct and return fire. Curt was right, Foster thought, it seemed damned lame for them to play this game.

"Orders are orders, buddy-boy. If Lippman says play punching bag, that's what we do. Don't sweat your career, the director's been informed, and we'll make out like bandits if we pull this off."

Bannion tensed as the door swung open. Behind it he saw the figure of a man who looked as if he might have been a boxer at one time. For a brief moment their eyes met, then Bannion was moving.

• • •

Foster took a deep breath, and opened the door. The red hood covering Mike's head shocked him, its terrorist association activating his professional reactions despite a conscious recognition otherwise. As his gun hand began to sweep the suit coat back from his empty holster, Bannion's .45 crashed into his face, breaking his nose and sending a thick spray of bright red blood across the opposite wall.

Staggering, Foster attempted to say something but was cut off when Bannion booted him between the legs. Falling to the carpet and rolling onto his belly, the agent shuddered as he felt one, then two bullets thud into his protected back. The pain from the gunshots was like that of being hit with a baseball bat; dull yet convincing. He lay still, watching through tearing eyes as a pair of rubber-soled boots stepped over him, heading for the living room. An involuntary spasm rushed through his body when the hand found the thick artery running up the outside of his throat, its fingers apparently checking his rapidly beating pulse. "You're fine," whispered the disembodied voice, "just stay down and we'll be outta here in minute or so." Then a second set of boots stepped over his head, following those of the man whose silenced pistol Foster could hear slapping rounds into Curt's vest-encased upper body.

He wanted to laugh, but knew it would hurt too much. He should have let Curt answer the door like he'd wanted to. The point man *always* draws fire, Foster remembered from his tour in Vietnam. While his broken face continued to ooze and burp blood, he reminded himself to *never* volunteer again, then he passed out.

Bannion burst into the spacious living room, pistol at the ready, then tracking fast as he locked onto his next target. The reed-thin agent on the couch jumped up like a startled deer, thrusting his hands out in front of his body as if they could ward off the gunner's low-velocity intentions by themselves. Unable to adjust his sight picture, Bannion's first round tore a huge chuck of flesh from Curt's open hand, then buried itself in his chest. The impact knocked the man ass-backward onto the couch, Bannion's second slow-mover striking just above the belly button. Still trying to escape his hooded assailant's line of fire, Curt pushed himself forward and onto the floor. For his effort, Bannion caught him in the ribs with a full-power karate kick. Both men heard several of the fragile bones snap like kindling, then the agent was down and out for the count.

Thornton, ignoring the passion play taking place between Bannion and the FBI man, rushed through the living room. He paused a moment, listening for the third agent, then, hearing nothing, headed for the conference room where the Montalvos were waiting. Abruptly a door on his left opened just as he passed it, bright light flooding the narrow hallway, a man in a white shirt, shoulder holster, and red tie looking at him in shocked amazement.

Bo noted that the agent's handgun was still in its holster. Without hesitation, he delivered a stinging knuckle chop to the man's throat. The agent gagged as the blow connected, his trachea constricting from the force of Thornton's well-aimed chop. Before he could slam the door, the apparition which greeted him after his healthy shit shoved him face first into the toilet bowl.

Ordering himself not to struggle, the agent felt his revolver ripped away from the Ted Blocker holster under his right armpit. He heard the cylinder snapped open, then the plunger slapped as six magnum rounds were ejected into the sink next to him. His sphincter shrunk itself into a tight ball when the man spoke, the words sounding as if they were being dragged over a bed of razors.

"You stupid son of a bitch! When this is over I'll have your fucking ass! No guns! No bullets! I'll just bet you were in the bathroom jacking off when the word was put out!"

A hand grabbed a wad of his thick hair, yanking his head out of the toilet's freshly flushed interior. Hearing the vertebrae in his neck pop as they hyper-extended, the agent found himself looking into a pair of eyes that seemed devoid of anything even remotely human. "I-I-I'm sorry," he whined, knowing his apology was useless at this point.

"Yes. Yes, you are indeed sorry, but that's Lippman's problem, not mine," the voice intoned. "Time to go to sleep . . . asshole!" Thornton, releasing the man's hair, shifted his hand so he now held the agent by the shirt collar. Slipping his other hand underneath the agent's alligator belt, the powerful night fighter stood up, holding the agent as if he were an oddly shaped suitcase. Arms bulging, Thornton stepped back into the deserted passageway, then ran forward, ramming the man's forehead into the tiled basin.

Dropping the limp figure, Thornton wiped his gloved hands on his pants, then ran to where he was to meet Ricardo and his anxious family.

Stopping to pull his mask off before entering, Thornton shook his head, smoothing his hair with one hand. Slipping into the room, he found Montalvo sitting next to his wife, their daughter standing at the double glass doors leading onto the balcony. As the girl turned so that he could see her fully, Thornton exhaled in appreciation. Maritza Montalvo was a beauty. Her chiseled Latin features were framed in shoulder-length black hair, pulled back and tied with a purple ribbon. She wore a black sweater which accented the mounds of her breasts, small but firm in a pouting way. Dark blue Levis encased a colt's long legs, her ass shaped like a pear ripe for the picking. She wore ankle-high jogging shoes with a British flag on their sides, and an amused look in her dark eyes.

Nodding in her direction, Bo turned his attention to Montalvo, who was gathering his and his wife's coats from a table in front of them. "We need to hurry, *señor*," he said in Spanish, "please avoid looking at the FBI men as we leave. They are not seriously hurt, but I'm afraid there is some blood."

"We are used to blood, Mr. Thornton," the girl responded. "A little more isn't going to shock us, isn't that so, *mi papa*?"

Montalvo, his arm around his wife, gestured for the girl to follow. Looking up at Thornton, he said, "She would like you to believe her fearless, Bo. But her heart beats as fast as mine right now."

Ushering the family into the corridor, Bo felt an electric charge run through him as the girl brushed up against his chest. "Would you like to feel how fast my heart is beating, Mr. Thornton?" she asked in a whisper. Then she was gone, following her father and mother down the hall to where Bannion, still wearing his hood, was waiting for them.

"Holy shit, where do these young girls *come* from?" Bo asked himself. Pausing for a moment to check the busted-up agent in the bathroom, Thornton retraced his steps through the living room and back into the hallway where Silver stood outside the elevator's open doors.

"Where's Lippman?" Thornton whispered.

"I dragged his ass into the apartment and left it on the kitchen floor. He'll be okay." Silver didn't add that before exiting the kitchen he'd delivered another boot to Lippman's already-swollen nut sack.

Bannion was stuffing the silencer back into his jacket, the .45's magazine well now holding a full complement of Remington Silver Tips rather than the stepped-down loads he'd used on the FBI. It was then that Thornton realized the back of Mike's jacket was silk screened, the words reading "Soldier of Fortune World Tour," an image of a globe with individual countries mapped out and named, sparkling in the light of the elevator's neon bars.

"How's everyone?" asked Bo as the doors glided shut.

"I am fine, Señor Thornton," replied Montalvo's wife. It was the first time Bo had heard the woman say anything since the breakout. Her voice was low and even, pleasing in its tone, cultured in its precise selection of words.

"I'm happy to hear that, señora. We will be at Father Delgado's church within the hour. He's excited about your arrival, and I understand he's prepared some food and a place to rest after you've talked."

The older woman smiled, her face brightening at the mention of the priest's name. "I wish only to pray, to give thanks to our Holy Father, then I will think of eating and sleeping." Turning to her husband, she squeezed his arm, then laid her head against his chest.

Bannion punched override, then the button that would take them to the third floor. Removing his mask, but not his gloves, the DEA agent gave Maritza Montalvo a good going-over. It was apparent that he approved of what he saw.

It was equally obvious that she did, too.

Before the doors were fully opened, Bo led the team into the hallway. The only people present were partygoers standing at the opposite end of the long corridor. They barely noticed the small group as Thornton opened the door to the stairwell, engrossed as they were with their own self-importance. Minutes later, Silver peered across the expanse of the underground garage which provided parking for the hotel's paying guests. Satisfied it was clear, he motioned to the others, who were waiting one landing above him.

Breaking them into two groups, Thornton reminded Jason and Bannion to look for Hartung's blue van. Then Bannion, Mrs. Montalvo, and Maritza strolled across the garage and into the night. Waiting a few moments, Thornton signaled Silver to do the same with Ricardo Montalvo, the two disappearing as quickly as the first group had. Thornton waited a few moments longer, then followed. He would act as their tail gunner, pulling drag in case they were followed or intercepted by an unknown and unexpected force. Thornton had learned that one never took anything for granted when walking among wolves. To do so was to invite death, and death always accepted invitations.

Ten minutes later, he watched Bannion and his group climb into the sergeant major's waiting van. Soon afterward, one block down, Silver and his ward did the same. Thornton quickly unlocked the door of the rented Thunderbird he had stashed on the street earlier. Pulling in behind the van, he checked his mirrors and pulled a walkie-talkie from underneath the seat. Switching it on, he keyed the mike twice, receiving an immediate acknowledgment from Hartung in the van.

"Take us home, Pappy. We're good to go from where I sit," said Thornton.

"Roger that," came the static-shrouded reply. "See you in church."

The penthouse was quiet. The apartment's door had been shut and locked when the team departed, leaving only the decimated FBI men inside. In the kitchen, Richard Lippman struggled to regain consciousness. Eyes fluttering, he rolled over on his back, jerking his knees up to his stomach as the pain from his groin convulsed him. Slowly, carefully, almost lovingly he moved his hands down to where his balls were throbbing in a state of pain so profound he felt tears coursing down his cheeks. He'd expected to be knocked out, had even wondered what the experience would be like. But he couldn't have imagined having his testicles used like a hockey team's doormat. Pushing one hand into his pants, Lippman gently cupped his battered balls, then passed out as a fresh wave of gut-knotting pain exploded inside his pounding skull.

CHAPTER

10

"We got anything from the remote unit yet?"

"Just a sec, let me run that by Tony. Hey, Tony . . . you heard from the remote over at the hotel yet?"

"Yeah, they just finished shooting some footage with the ambulances leaving. Jane says it's a real mess out there, but she got some good stuff for tonight's broadcast."

"Great! I'll pass that along to Brad. What about our people over at the church?"

"Dunno about that. Give Chris a shout, she pulled the crew for the Delgado thing."

"Okay, will do. When you've got the Fairmont tape, give me a holler, we'll want to preview it, maybe go back to back with whatever Chris gets. Brad wants to do a teaser on the noon news, with an in-depth follow-up tonight at six."

"You got it. Hey, can you believe the FBI fucked up like this?"

"Sure, why not? Look what happened to them in Florida. You start believing your own press, and we'll get you every time."

"Father Delgado? I'm Chris Avila, KBRK News. Can you tell us when exactly the Montalvos met with you?"

The priest, with infinite patience, studied his newest questioner. He recognized her as one of the more successful Latina broadcast personalities working in the Bay Area. She was much prettier than many of the reporters and journalists who were crowded into the small room he'd chosen for the press conference, but then not many people were blessed with looks, talent, and good fortune.

"Ricardo Montalvo brought his family to the church before morning prayers were to begin," Delgado paused, snuffing out his cigarette in the single ashtray set before him. "As I told you, Señor Montalvo and I are old friends; I am honored he came to me for help."

"Father Delgado! Matt Simpson from the *Chronicle*. Is it true that Montalvo escaped from FBI custody with help from the PPF, the same revolutionary group President Aguilar holds responsible for the massacre of fifty peasants in his country three weeks ago?"

"No, that is not true." Delgado swung his head toward the opposite side of the room, hoping for a question that made sense. These reporters, he thought to himself, are they really as ignorant as they present themselves?

"Father . . . Ray Phillips of the *Berkeley Free Press*. Do *you* know who engineered this attack against the FBI, and if so, would you enlighten us?"

"Señor Montalvo explained to me that three men wearing red hoods and gloves broke into the apartment, and after attacking their FBI guards, forced them from the hotel—"

"Were they armed, Father?"

"Were *who* armed? The attackers? The FBI? The Montalvos? You will have to be more explicit with your questions, my son. Remember that I am only one of God's humble servants, and clarity is one of the things I seek."

The reporter, an overweight freelancer from San Jose who needed a fast story to pay his rent, rephrased the question, ignoring the laughter of his peers. "Sorry, Father. Were the terrorists armed, is what I meant."

"Yes. The Montalvos were very frightened, and are concerned about the well-being of the agents who were responsible for their safety."

"Father Delgado . . ."

It was the Latin woman again, he would defer to her because KBRK was an affiliate of one of the major networks. They could use the national coverage. "Yes, my daughter?"

"Father, how did the Montalvos escape from their abductors, and why?"

"I only know they were forced into a van and driven toward the Golden Gate. Along the way the driver lost control—Ricardo believes because the street was wet and the driver was in too much of a hurry—and the van went off the road. The family was able to get out of the vehicle and flag down a passing taxi, which they took to an all-night diner on the wharf. They waited there until light, then came to the church."

"Sir, a follow-up to my question! Does Ricardo Montalvo know who these people were?"

Delgado felt it was time. Looking to his left, he saw Ricardo was ready, standing just out of sight from the press people. With a nod, the priest signaled his understanding, then focused his attentions once again on the reporter. "I cannot answer that, my dear. But Señor Montalvo can, and it is my sincere pleasure to introduce him to you at this time."

Hand-held cameras captured the man as he walked briskly across the tiny stage, stopping to genuflect before the priest, kissing his ring in reverence for the Holy Father. Ricardo Montalvo turned and faced the group, taking a seat next to Delgado only when the flood of questions threatened to sweep him away. On either side of the stage, just out of sight, stood Thornton and Bannion. Both men were carrying submachine guns under their jackets, as well as their heavy pistols.

"My friends," Montalvo began, "I am most pleased you could take the time to attend this press conference. I will answer what questions I can, but please be brief, as I am very tired and still have much to discuss with the good father."

A hand flew up from the middle of the crowd. "Sir, is your family all right, and where are they now?"

Flash units exploded in his eyes, their abruptness punctuating the hot white glare coming from the television cameras' portable light sources. Along with a gaggle of microphones set before him, Montalvo faced a battery of hand-held tape recorders and boom mikes. For a moment he was tempted to simply leave, but remembering how necessary it was for them to inform his people in La Libertad that he was alive and well, he stayed.

Hands folded in front of him, Montalvo stole a quick glance at

Thornton, who gave the throng of reporters a one-finger salute, bringing a smile to the Latin's face. "My wife and daughter are safe. None of us was hurt in any way during the attack. We have asked Father Delgado to extend to us the right of sanctuary in his church, and he has done so. We will be staying here for the time being."

A loud voice from the rear of the audience erupted. "Señor Montalvo, has the United States State Department been in contact with you since learning of your presence here?"

"No. I expect they will be, though. You see, we do not have our visas with us . . ."

A sprinkle of laughter carried across the room. Then the questions began again.

"Ricardo, Ricardo Montalvo! Are you responsible for the deaths of fifty Libertadian nationalists, as President Aguilar has claimed? And if so, don't you think it a sacrilege to seek protection from the church?"

Thornton recognized the fire in Montalvo's eyes as he listened to the reporter. This should be good, Bo thought. Leave it to the media to get shitty when they need something to suck the viewers in.

"The slaughter you mention was one which was planned and carried out by the president of La Libertad through his secret police. My family and I were to have bene murdered along with those who did die, and we would have been had not God intervened. If there is responsibility for the dead, it lies upon the shoulders of the president, and the jackals who do his killing for him!"

"Do you know who tried to kidnap you last night?" The question came from a gangly young reporter, probably representing one of the college newspapers.

Montalvo ran a hand through his hair. He felt himself fading, surprised that the events of the night before should have taken so much from him. "No. They did not identify themselves. Whoever it was that forced us to take this avenue, they were not our friends, or our supporters."

"*Señor*, Raul Garcia Lopez of the *Latin Daily*. Would you return to FBI custody if it were offered?"

"Not at this time. If the FBI couldn't protect us where we

were, how can I expect them to do so now? No. We will take our chances with Father Delgado until a decision is made concerning our plea for political asylum."

Delgado stood, his hands raised to quiet the mass of reporters who were beginning to press forward. "Please, please! Only one more question, then I must insist that Señor Montalvo rest." Looking for the television woman, he found her close by. "Señorita Avila? Perhaps you would pose the final question?"

The attractive anchorwoman mouthed a silent Hail Mary for priests whose vow of celibacy didn't interfere with their eye for beauty. Edging forward, dragging her cameraman behind, she was able to get close enough to Montalvo for a close-up. "Señor Montalvo . . . the PPF controls the entire eastern portion of your country, President Aguilar has vowed not to step down, nor to bargain with the guerrillas. You are rumored to be a heavy favorite if the U.S.-sponsored elections can be held. Will you run if that happens, and what will be your plans if you win?"

Montalvo leaned forward, his mineral blue eyes meeting the cold lens of the camera, the words he chose so firmly spoken there could be no mistake as to his message. The room fell silent as he addressed them, their recorders and note pads idle. Thornton, in the eaves, caught Bannion's attention. They couldn't become caught up in what was happening, although it was difficult not to succumb to the power of the man. Bannion nodded his understanding. Thornton glimpsed Maritza Montalvo standing next to the deadly SLAM technician, her left hand placed gently over the agent's right shoulder, a South American gesture indicating she was with her man. Bo shook his head, oh to be young again, he thought. Montalvo's words drew him back.

". . . I have met with, and know well, the leadership of the PPF. We have agreed to disagree on many things. Aguilar insists that I am somehow a member of this organization, a guerrilla commander or something. I am not now, nor have I ever been so associated with the guerrillas.

"The war in my country has taken many lives on all sides. Six years of killing has not brought about peace, it has only brought about more killing. The PPF is dedicated to a Communist-style government in La Libertad. They have told me this. I do not believe such a form of government is what the people want.

Aguilar is dedicated to maintaining himself in power. He is as Somoza was in Nicaragua, a brutal dictator whose wealth and power is fed by the labor of his subjects. He, also, is not what my people want.

"*If* the United States carries out its promise of elections, I will accept my party's nomination to run for the office of president. Naturally the PPF, if they are truly sure of their position, will do everything within their power to see those areas under their control enjoy the opportunity to participate freely in casting their votes. The same holds true for Aguilar. Let us see who and what the people of La Libertad choose."

"And if they choose you, *señor*, what will you do once you are in office?" Chris asked, the camera fading from her back to Montalvo.

Montalvo turned up his intensity, his eyes reflecting every sorrow, every hurt, every seed of hope that was lying dormant in the suddenly strategic country of La Libertad. "I would order an immediate cease-fire, which, if not adhered to, would be followed by a request to the United Nations for a peace-keeping force. The army would be reorganized, those who have abused their uniform would be removed from service, and tried by court martial if crimes against the people are suspected. Aguilar and his cronies will be sent into exile, without the comfort of their wealth.

"All of our meager resources must be plowed into the rebuilding of the nation's economy. To do this I will encourage foreign investment, but only those investments which are fair and legal. We would not accept aid from countries whose intentions were suspect, or who are supporting baseless revolutions abroad. Our goal must be to rebuild, to reunite, to rethink our destiny in the affairs of Latin America!

"That is what I would do, if it is what my people want of me."

As Montalvo and Father Delgado exited the stage amid a flurry of questions, Thornton shook his head in wonder. Maybe we've got something here, he silently reflected. If so, we'd better start working overtime to keep Ricardo's ass alive, because when Aguilar gets wind of this hoedown, the shit's going to hit the fan!

CHAPTER

11

The rattle of firing reached Melendez's ears; short bursts from the assault rifles overridden by longer, more powerful ones from light machine guns. His battalion had been in contact with the guerrillas for two days, an amount of time unheard of six months ago. Melendez pondered that fact for a moment, knowing it meant the enemy was comfortable going toe to toe with the army.

And lately, more often than not, they were winning.

Melendez squatted under a low-hanging tree. His hands were wrapped around the Galil's front stock so his boot heels and the rifle's butt formed a tripod for him to rest on. Two Guatemalan mercenaries were pulling flank security on either side of the hard-barked tree, their rifles held loosely. Taking a lesson from Special Forces' preference for Chinese Nung mercs, Melendez hired the Guats to provide the level of security only money can buy. These two were hardened veterans of their own country's bitter insurgency.

The heat bore down on the three men with the fury only a tropical sun can muster. The dust beneath their feet was khaki brown, loose and fine as powdered sugar. Every bush and tree seemed armored with thick heavy bark, or needle-pointed thorns. The soldiers breathed like lizards, using slow, shallow inhalations to ventilate their lungs.

Consulting his watch, the major frowned, noting that it was nearing 1400 hours, wondering if he'd gotten Aguilar's message correctly from the teenage radioman. Adjusting himself slightly, then checking to ensure his fatigue pants were pulled well forward, Melendez continued his shit. He hadn't taken one since their forward element's near ambush forty-eight hours earlier. Since then the battalion had been constantly engaged, with Melendez's two platoons of reconnaissance teams running missions for Colonel Quevar at a breakneck pace. There wasn't time to eat or sleep, not to mention taking a healthy dump.

Melendez was curious as to why Aguilar would risk flying in to what was now the hottest combat action along the eastern front. Especially since he'd directed Melendez to meet him alone. He'd heard nothing from Aguilar since the president's personally signed transfer orders had taken him back to a combat unit, a "reward" for the disaster at El Refugio. At least I'm alive, he thought. Combat duty might have been punishment to some, to Melendez it was sweet nectar.

Three helicopters, one loach and two Hueys, shrieked directly over the hidden group, skids no more than fifteen feet above the ground. Their line of flight had been masked by a small hill, none of the group hearing the pilots' approach until the gunships crested the ridge, their rotors pounding heavily against thin air.

Melendez grimaced as his stomach muscles involuntarily contracted, the unexpected flush of adrenaline snapping through him like a surge of raw electricity. Damn! he inwardly cursed. Leave it to Aguilar to catch him with his pants down!

Raising himself to a half-crouch so he could tactically fasten his trousers, Melendez motioned to the two mercenaries that he was ready to meet the circling choppers. Choosing to wait until the escort ships assumed a protective 360-degree orbit, he pulled a swatch of international Orange parachute silk from a cargo pocket. Gripping it between both hands, Melendez stepped out from underneath the team's cover and began popping the signal panel at Aguilar's armed loach.

The pilot spotted their position almost immediately. Adjusting his rate and direction of descent, he coasted forward, covering the three hundred meters between them in little less than thirty seconds. Five hundred feet above, the escort ships bucked and dipped as they fought the air currents. Melendez could see door gunners leaning out against their safety harnesses, twin-barreled M-60s held tightly by their butterfly triggers while the helmeted gunners swept the terrain below for a target.

The loach settled onto the hard-packed earth with a soft

bump. Melendez whistled appreciatively at the GE Gatling gun mounted below the pilot's door. Its electric-driven swivel mount gave the gun a wide range of maneuver, the speed and agility of the loach making the entire system superbly practical for the kind of war they were fighting.

As the chopper's blades decelerated, the pilot popped his door open and stepped down using the single step bolted onto the loach's skid. Melendez recognized the aircraft commander as President Aguilar himself, even though the man was wearing an issue flight suit with the insignia of an Air Force colonel prominently displayed. The major watched the copilot's door open as Aguilar's bodyguard slipped from his seat. The man was a Salvadoran national, formerly a sergeant with that country's elite PRAL reconnaissance company. He wore tiger-stripe fatigues, a well-equipped combat harness, and carried a Styer-Aug assault rifle, easily recognized by its toad green bull-pup stock. Known only as Azo, the Salvadoran was rumored to wear a necklace made from over fifty human finger bones. Melendez would have liked to have confirmed the story, his own boonie hat was upholstered with a scalp taken after his first firefight.

Azo nodded at the two Guat soldiers of fortune, then slipped off to one side, where he could watch Aguilar but still keep out of the sun. Snapping his fingers twice, Melendez ordered his own chain dogs back on perimeter alert. Overhead, the remaining two helicopters circled them like dragonflies over a lily pad, their plexiglass snouts reflecting the sun's harsh glare, reminding Melendez of aluminum moths which were incapable of melting no matter how close they flew to the blistering orb.

"*Hola*, Luis. And how is my bushmaster liking his field assignment?" Aguilar came to a stop paces from where Melendez waited under the sparse shade the trees provided. His eyes were covered by dark green lenses, the RayBans a favorite among La Libertad's combat pilots. Securely strapped across his chest was a nickel-plated Colt .45, a spare magazine taped to the holster's front.

Melendez pushed an index finger against one nostril, blowing hard so that a slick gob of snot smacked the ground in a puff of dust. "It is better than listening to the whining of some fat-assed staff officer, or attending one of the many boring parties the president is expected to give every time some American senator conducts a 'fact-finding tour.' "

Aguilar chuckled, taking in the condition of Melendez's uniform. Its elbows were torn from crawling across sharp bits of lava. There was a splotch of dried blood on one side of the camouflaged battle tunic, human hair crusted into place where part of a soldier's skull had bounced off the major earlier that morning. The ammonialike smell of sweat permeated the air around Melendez, a bad perfume. Scuffed jungle boots testified to the roughness of the terrain the battalion was fighting in, a Gerber boot knife securely tucked into the right boot's canvas upper. Completing his battle wear was the major's dusky jungle hat, its broad brim jutting out from his oily forehead, and the Stabo combat harness. The harness alone must weigh fifty pounds, thought Aguilar as he mentally counted the number of ammunition pouches attached to its thick webbed belt.

Clapping the battle-hardened officer on the shoulder, Aguilar guided him farther under the tree. "The battle, it goes well for us?" he asked.

Shifting the Israeli assault rifle, Melendez paused to weigh his answer. Deciding he could lose nothing by telling the man the truth, he offered his opinion. "We have pushed the guerrillas into a series of arroyos and ravines since this morning's assault. For every one of the bastards we dig out, we end up losing three of our own. The terrain is a maze of caves, ledges, hollows, and cracks. It's the worst kind of close-in fighting you can imagine."

Aguilar looked at the thickset commando with pensive eyes. "What more do you need to get the job done?"

Melendez coughed, wanting to suck down one of the last two full canteens of water he was carrying. "Wouldn't that be better asked of the battalion commander, *mi Colonel*?"

"If I wanted his opinion of the situation," retorted Aguilar, "I'd have put the question to him. Quevar is one of my best field officers, his battalion the most feared by the guerrillas, but sometimes it is wiser to ask a subordinate the critical questions. Don't you agree, Major?"

Melendez looked up as a burst of machine-gun fire tore into the ridgeline, one of the Hueys making an abrupt turn and coming in low for another try at the unseen targets. "We need water and bullets. If the paratroopers are sober, they would be of use coming in from above the cliffs. Should we get this support, Quevar could begin mopping up within, say, two days. If not . . ."

Aguilar waved a gloved hand, cutting Melendez off. "I know, I know. 'If not,' the Communists will slither away like the snakes they are. Quevar will suffer unnecessary casualties, and we will not have won a conclusive victory. Once I am airborne, I will radio the airbase to scramble the paras. Water will be brought in by helicopter, but you'll probably get the bullets first. Anything else?"

Melendez shook his head.

"Good. Now, who do you think I saw on television this morning?"

A blank look crossed the major's features. Sensing it had something to do with Aguilar's being here, he shrugged his shoulders, a scab of hair breaking free from where it was stuck to his combat tunic and falling silently to the ground.

"Our old political friends, Father Delgado and Ricardo Montalvo." Aguilar waited patiently for Melendez's reaction to the news. It was because of Montalvo's escape that the major was in the field fighting for his life. Aguilar wanted it that way, knowing it would hone the man's brutal instinct for revenge should the opportunity become available.

"Two queers who suck the cock of world Communism," said Melendez. "It does not surprise me that they have decided to share the same bed."

"Yesterday someone 'helped' Montalvo to escape his FBI wardens. The priest has given the family sanctuary in his church while the U.S. State Department wrings its hands at this recent 'development.'

"Myself, I am leery of Ricardo's good fortune. No one has claimed credit for the act, and the gringos were to have turned the family over to our embassy this morning, something they now obviously cannot do. It is good timing for everyone but us, wouldn't you agree?"

Melendez nodded. He chose to remain silent, knowing Aguilar would make his point soon. A professional soldier lived only to carry out his orders. Knowing when to be quiet and listen were mandatory requirements to the success of any mission. He sensed

Aguilar was building a foundation for him, brick by brick. It didn't matter to him if he left the field or not, combat was far more enjoyable than slaughtering political malcontents. But if the president were to offer him a second chance at Montalvo . . . well, the war would always be here when he returned.

The gunships began engaging more targets on the backside of the ridge, their urgency telling Aguilar that he needed to get airborne soon or chance coming under fire. "I should have known that sending you to Quevar was a gift rather than punishment for the fiasco at El Refugio. A military attaché's desk in Togo would have brought you to your knees, or maybe an instructor's position at the academy. You would have hated *that*." Both men laughed, knowing the truth of Aguilar's words. Bracing Melendez with a look capable of igniting fires, Aguilar's mood changed as swiftly as a woman's mind. "The gringos are playing a dangerous game with me. I must have Montalvo dead before the elections. I want you to take a team to the United States. Find Montalvo and kill him. Should you succeed, I have your promotion papers signed and waiting on my desk. . . . If not, you will again be carrying a rifle into combat, but as a sergeant!"

A grenade exploded somewhere to the west of them. "When do I leave?" asked Melendez.

Aguilar signaled the Salvadoran to return to the loach. "Now. I'll send one of the Hueys down as soon as I can cover you from the air. There's a TACA flight leaving for Dallas tomorrow morning. You and your men will be on it. Your arrangements have been made by my staff. By tomorrow evening you'll be in San Francisco."

"I want my Guats, no one else. A problem?"

"No. Just have our people dummy up some diplomatic passports for them. I take it they are effective?"

Melendez, checking his rifle's safety, answered, "I don't know. They haven't left anyone alive long enough for me to ask."

Aguilar slapped his thigh in appreciation. "*Adios*, Major. I'll see you before you leave. Enjoy the flight, although we may spend some time testing the new gun on the *subersivos* before heading back." Turning, Aguilar ran to the all-black loach and strapped himself back into the pilot's seat. The high-pitched whine of the starter motor began to howl as the blades slowly picked up speed. In seconds the chopper's turbine coughed to life, its power whipping the main rotor to a frenzy, lifting dirt, rocks, and small branches off the ground and throwing them helter-skelter across the LZ.

As the bird lifted off, Melendez acknowledged the president's nod with a wave of his own. Then the gunship was gone, racing for altitude, the Gatling gun turning on axis, its deadly multi-barrel snout eager to churn living flesh and bone into soggy mush. The major shouted for the two mercenaries to join him. He could already see one of the slicks breaking out of its orbit and heading for them. One of the Guats touched his shoulder and pointed to the ridgeline where Aguilar was making a gun run. The tiny loach was less than a hundred feet off the deck and flying at over one hundred knots. Suddenly the ground in front of the airship began to erupt as the ripsaw sound of the Gatling gun reached their ears. Pulling hard against the stick, Aguilar pointed the chopper's nose straight up as he broke off his attack against the unseen targets.

Stuffing his boonie hat into a cargo pocket, Melendez bent low against the force of the Huey's rotor wash and ran for its open door. The mercs waited until he'd leaped onto the aluminum-plated deck before making their way to the extraction ship. When they were all on board, the pilot gave a thumbs-up to the crew chief, bringing the gunship up and around with a subtle combination of moves, using his cyclic and collective controls. From their increased vantage point, Melendez could watch the loach's repeated attacks against the men scurrying for cover below them. Bright blots of blood showed where the Gatling gun's rounds had struck home. The guerrillas vainly attempt to return fire with their assault rifles, unable to do so effectively because of the quickness of the loach and the fury of its firepower.

Abruptly the loach peeled off, heading in the direction of the capital eighty miles away. The slicks fell in behind the skimming black waterbug, forming a flying wedge that swept across the sky with the arrogance of predatory birds. Behind them, the guerrillas were climbing out of their holes in preparation for the infantry attack they knew was coming from Quevar's battalion.

Melendez tucked himself up against the bird's fire wall and

stared out over the shoulder of a door gunner who was sweeping spent shell casings out of the ship with his boot. The Guats were already dozing, their heads bobbing with the roll of the ship as it rode the air currents. So, we will have the opportunity to meet again, Señor Montalvo. I think that this time you will not be so fortunate, Melendez thought to himself. Remembering the girl, he rubbed his filthy crotch without thinking. He would have to make a point of finding her also, such innocence and sweetness was a sin to ignore. The Guats could have the mother, something Melendez was sure they'd appreciate. The president believed that dangling the carrot of promotion in front of him would compel the major to succeed where before he had failed. Melendez snorted at the bribe, knowing he'd have taken the offer regardless of a colonel's commission. He *wanted* Montalvo's head. In fact, he would have the Communist's skull cured and fashioned into an attractive desk lamp like those he'd seen in Quevar's office.

It would be a fitting end for Señor Ricardo Montalvo. As for the girl . . . her hair would replace the worn scalp he'd taken so many months ago. Recalling the rich texture of her hair, he harbored no doubts that it would prove comfortable stitched inside the battered campaign hat.

The cool winds at that altitude washed over him, driving away the grit and dusty paste of the battlefield. Closing his eyes, he rested, the thought of Montalvo's throat in his hands causing a smile to form on his face.

To the crew chief sitting opposite the bearded major, the expression appeared grotesque, like that of a death head's leer straight from hell's deepest pit.

He shuddered, turning away from the camouflaged gargoyle's sneering features, reminded by the soldier's sour odor of how fortunate he was to be assigned to the Air Force. At least they could bathe every night. . . .

CHAPTER
12

"...that's what Billings told me this morning, Bo. I know it's crazy, but State is confident it will work." Calvin Bailey leaned back in the frail wooden chair, his powerful hands clasped behind his head. Watching Thornton's reaction to the news he'd just received, the DEA agent wondered if Lippman would live out the week. The man in front of him was a simmering volcano, ready to explode, and Bailey couldn't blame him.

Thornton stood and began pacing the small rectory Father Delgado had allowed them to use for their meetings. It was a simple room, the walls adorned with religious paintings; a tasteful icon picturing Christ on the cross hung from the back of the closed door. It was a peaceful setting, although both men felt the mystery of the Catholic faith all around them. It seemed praying and planning went hand in hand where the holy church was involved.

The grim-faced commando leader stopped to examine one of the paintings, then turned to Bailey. "I remember when Nixon was running for reelection, there was this graffiti written on one of the latrine walls in camp. It went. 'Vote for Nixon—Why Change Dicks in the Middle of a Butt-Fuck?' That's how I feel about what's going down now."

"For what it's worth, Billings is throwing a fit. He went as far as to ask for an appointment with the president...but with the bullshit hitting the fan about Iran, there isn't any way he can get in." Fishing a cigarette from the fresh pack he carried in his pocket, Bailey lit up, the smoke curling upward in the stillness of the room.

93

Thornton returned to his chair. He was just beginning to see the light at the end of the tunnel when Bailey arrived, telling him they needed to talk. The Montalvos were hidden away in quarters normally reserved for visiting clergy. Bannion and Silver stayed with them while Hartung and Bo shared a small room across from the dwelling. The atmosphere seemed to have calmed the family; even Mrs. Montalvo was beginning to behave as if she were a mother to them all.

"It's been two days since we moved the family here. Lippman didn't say *anything* about State having the option to change its mind. We're supposed to baby-sit the package for one week, one damned week! Easy shit. Now they want us to take out Aguilar's fucking hit team and *use* the Montalvos as bait! It's fucking insane, Cal, simply in-fucking-sane. . . ."

Bailey blew a perfect smoke ring, watching it float across the room, growing larger and larger until it finally fell apart. "Not to change the subject, but Lippman is croaking bloody murder about how bad he got stomped during our little escapade. He wants Jason's ass *bad*."

Thornton leaned forward, elbows on the table between the two men; when he spoke his voice held an evil tone. "If we were ruckin' on the back slope of this little party I'd consider addressing the matter. But, seeing as Lippman and company have changed dicks on us, I really don't give a shit about that scumbag's problem."

Bailey nodded in agreement. "Yeah, well he's going to be in the hospital for another three or four days from what I hear. They don't want to release him until his nuts stop glowing in the dark."

A ripple of soft laughter floated through the room as both men chortled to themselves.

"Okay, I feel better knowing that Lippman is paying his dues like the rest of us. Now, tell me again what the hell it is State has up its slimy sleeve."

Bailey ground the butt of his cigarette out on the table's top, forgetting the ashtray provided by the priests. Thornton didn't seem to notice the oversight, his mind wrestling with the enormity of the situation they now faced. He felt control of their destiny slipping away from him, and he didn't like the sensation.

Propping the cane between his legs and resting his chin atop the sword's butt, Bailey replayed the scenario sent down by State.

"One of the intel pogues working out of the embassy got word from a captain in Aguilar's palace guard that the president has dispatched a hit team. Supposedly they flew into Dallas yesterday morning on diplomatic passports. From there it appears they rented a private plane, and for all we know they could be in the city right now.

"This captain told our boy the *jefe* in charge is none other than Major Luis Melendez. . . ."

Bo interrupted, his interest peaked at the mention of Melendez's name. "*The* famous Major Melendez, butcher of El Refugio and all-around bad-ass?"

Calvin grinned. "As the man says, 'you got it, Toyota.' The major got his walking papers from Aguilar after Montalvo escaped. Seems he spent a few weeks popping caps at folks who could shoot back. This trip looks to be the president's way of saying Luis can wipe the slate clean . . . if he takes Montalvo out."

"Why the fuck let these bastards in, anyway? State obviously knows what their intentions are, why not deny them entry and go ahead with Plan A?"

Calvin left his chair, dragging the cane along behind him. He'd been awakened from a sound sleep by Billings's call at five that morning. Back in Washington it was already eight; Billings had come in an hour earlier for his meeting with the secretary. Reaching the door, Bailey shrugged his massive shoulders, wondering if he'd have time to get a workout in before the day ended. It had been a week since he'd last pumped iron, and the stress was beginning to get to him.

"The G's have secured the entire eastern half of La Libertad. As of yesterday some colonel named Quevar got his battalion waxed in what the reports say is the biggest ambush of the war. Seems the guerrillas tossed all their chips on the table and suckered this poor slob into the Libertadian version of Little Big Horn.

"Anyway, the political arm of the PPF is formally requesting they be recognized by the United Nations as a legal government. They are administrating the territory they control, and from a military standpoint, Aguilar can only conduct air attacks against targets in the region. With all three bridges down across the Rio Fuca, his armor and infantry are sitting on their asses.

"State is afraid the PPF will be recognized by the U.N. If that happens, and with Nicaragua and Cuba already promising to support the PPF at the assembly's meeting, there will be no reason for elections to be held. Aguilar will drag the war out until he's forced from power or dead, and Montalvo's worth to us rings up a big zero on the old political cash register as he becomes a non-player."

Thornton closed his eyes, rubbing his temples slowly, hoping to ease the headache he felt coming on. "Why do I feel I've seen this movie before?" he asked. "How the hell do I tell Ricardo that we're going to set him up so we can bring Aguilar down, that is, unless this Melendez asshole gets lucky and blows us all away."

Bailey strode back to where Bo was sitting. "That's the other thing State *doesn't* want done," he whispered. "Montalvo is not to know we're setting him up. He's got to believe we didn't know anything about it, that we just happened to respond in the appropriate manner. It sucks—I know that—but it's the way it has to be done."

Thornton leaped up from the table, pushing it hard away from him, his eyes blazing with frustration and anger. "That's bullshit, Cal! Plain, unadulterated bullshit! Who the fuck do they think they are? You don't pull a man out of a fire, then soak him down with gasoline and flick matches at him. Montalvo's *got* to know what's happening. It's *his* family, for God's sake!"

Bailey let the man simmer for a few moments. When Thornton appeared somewhat calmer, the drug buster spoke. "If you tell Montalvo, he'll throw a fit to State, maybe even go public with everything that's happened up to now. We'll deny anything he says and probably turn him over to Aguilar ASAP. If that happens, he's DO-fucking-A.

"On the other hand, if you run with the ball the way it is now, he has a chance to not only live, but to accomplish what he most wants to. If Springblade can intercept Melendez when he makes his attempt, State will have what it needs to put the pressure on Aguilar to step down. Montalvo will be able to walk right into the president's office and begin negotiations with the PPF while the U.S. stalls the U.N. vote with its veto.

"This is the last play in the coach's book, Bo. We either run it the way State tells us, or you guys can take your money and go home."

Thornton directed a white-hot look of hurt toward Bailey as the last remark hit home. "I'm no fucking mercenary, you bastard. That was a cheap shot, and I fucking well resent it, coming from you!"

Calvin leaned into the big man's face, his own frustration bubbling to the surface. "Then quit acting like some FNG who's never been here before! Shit, I like the Montalvos, too. They're decent people, and they've got a chance to change something that *can* be changed. But not unless you pull your stubborn head out your ass and start acting like a professional about this.

"You know the score. We did the same thing to the 'Yards in Nam. Won their hearts and minds, then left them to face the music when we pulled out. Same story with the Shah and his boys. Somoza paid the piper, and the Contras would have, too, if it hadn't been for Ronbo and Ollie North. Well, Montalvo's in a world of shit if *we* don't get behind this fucked-up plan of State's. It's his only shot, Bo . . . his only fucking shot."

Bailey watched Thornton's murderous gaze begin to soften. Inside he was cold as ice, wondering if he hadn't gone too far. They both knew the former Beret could pull his team and walk. That was the deal between him and the president; Springblade ran the missions given them, the missions didn't run them. Calvin knew what would happen if Bo threw in the towel; Melendez would get Montalvo. Everything in the man's background showed him to be a sure-thing kinda guy.

When Thornton spoke, his voice was low, its tone bridging the gap that had opened between them. "You got balls, squid, I'll give that to you. Time was when I'd kick a man's ass who talked to me like that . . . unless he outranked me, that is. But you said your piece, and damn me if it doesn't make sense. Took balls, though."

Bailey stepped back from the table, grinning. "My balls as big as Lippman's?" he teased.

"Shit!" Thornton barked, "the Jolly Green fucking Giant ain't got a pair as big as Lippman's after Jason's little tap-dancing session!"

"Friends?" asked Bailey, extending his hand toward Thornton.

"Was there ever any doubt . . . asshole?"

The two gripped each other's hands so hard their knuckles popped. Breaking contact, they looked around the room sheepishly, as if they might find something the other had lost. Regaining their composure, both policed up their equipment and prepared to leave. Bailey stopped Thornton at the door, his hand on his shoulder.

"What are you going to say to Montalvo?"

Bo's answer was immediate. "I'm going to tell him everything looks good so far. We'll tighten up our coverage, Frank and I will move in with everyone so we're all under one roof. If possible, see if you can get me two extra S.F.P.D. units to cover the streets. They won't be able to stop Melendez when he makes his move, but they may slow him down long enough for us to meet him halfway."

Bailey nodded. "What about Delgado?"

"He's an activist, so we'll have to watch him closely. I don't think Aguilar will be interested in him as long as he isn't within shooting range. Up until now he hasn't shown much interest in the team, and I'd like to keep it that way."

"Fine with me. I'll call Billings and let him know what we've decided. Lippman wants to see me this afternoon, so I'll swing by the hospital and powwow with him. Probably get back to you early this evening."

"Roger that, Cal. I'm gonna get together with the team after I shoot the shit with Ricardo over lunch. Talk to you later . . . Oh, by the way, give Dick Lips our best when you see him."

"And make his day?" Bailey chided. "No way, my man, no motherfuckin' way."

Thornton joined Montalvo an hour later on the small patio in front of their quarters. From their table they watched a steady stream of worshipers and visitors who entered the church. Since Father Delgado's arrival, he'd embarked on a restoration project that resulted in the church being able to boast having the most beautiful gardens and walkways of any in the city. The house the

Montalvos occupied sat in the farthest corner of the property, its front hidden from view by a hedgerow over ten feet in height. A narrow walkway gave entrance, with only a wrought-iron gate to deny unwanted visitors access.

From where the patio stood, Montalvo and Thornton could see the huge fountain sitting in the middle of the square. Its arcing jets of water drew crowds that gathered around, tossing coins into the shallow depths, adding wishes to their prayers. It was a peaceful scene, enhanced by the balmy day's temperature and a gentle breeze coming off the bay.

"You are well, Bo?" asked Montalvo as he buttered a thick piece of French bread, freshly baked that morning.

"Well enough, considering the situation, Ricardo." Thornton raised a glass of iced tea to his lips.

"Your people are very good. I am impressed especially by the sergeant major. It's hard to believe one man can have been to so many places in a single lifetime."

Bo set the glass back on the varnished tabletop. "Yeah, Frank's seen the bear and barked at the moon. Not many like him left anymore."

Montalvo laughed, the sound light and airy against the bright afternoon's sun. "If I become president, I may hire him away from you. His insight is most refreshing."

Thornton joined in the laughter. "Yes, the sergeant major's got specific views about the world we live in. You'd better pay him on time, and in full, though. He's the kind of 'consultant' that can either keep you in power, or remove you, depending on how you pay your bills."

Looking around but not seeing Montalvo's wife, Bo asked if she was feeling better.

"Oh, *la señora* is fine, my friend," replied Montalvo, finishing a bowl of chicken soup. "In fact, she is with Father Delgado, who is helping some unfortunate children to learn how to read English. They are also part of the sanctuary process, and come from mostly Guatemala and El Salvador."

"My men are not in your way, I trust?"

Waving his spoon in front of him, the Latino finished a mouthful of food before answering. "No, of course not. The one called Bannion is as gentle as he is dangerous, and I'm afraid

Maritza is quite in love with him. I haven't heard her laugh so easily since our escape from the arroyo, and she acts like a girl her age should.

"Silver, he is a madman, no?"

Thornton shook his head yes.

"Ah, you know what I mean, then? The man is always telling me jokes, and playing pranks on the women. He is one tough *hombre*, though, I can see it in his eyes whenever there is a strange sound in the house, or visitors who stray too close to the gate."

Bo grunted. "Yeah, Jason spent two tours in Vietnam. He's a little *loco*, but you needn't worry about his ability. If push came to shove, he'd be right up front gettin' some."

The bell for chapel began to ring, its melody drawing some of the crowd from the fountain toward the open doors of the church. Thornton studied the square, looking for someone who didn't fit in, someone who wasn't interested in wishes or hymns, someone whose religion was violent death.

He could see no one that fit the bill.

"How are the FBI men?" asked Montalvo. Thornton made note of the fact that he didn't inquire about Lippman's condition.

"Fine, more or less. Bailey tells me they'll be released from the hospital in a few days, then shuttled back to D.C." He paused for a moment, then added, "We didn't rough them up too bad, Ricardo."

"I know you did only what was necessary, Bo. Silver tells me that Lippman may not father children, though."

With a spark of mischief in his eyes, Thornton muttered just loud enough for his luncheon companion to hear. "That may be a blessing, Ricardo. Can you imagine what any children of Lippman's would be like?"

Montalvo laughed. "Can you imagine what the *woman* who would bear such children would be like?" he asked in mock horror.

Both men shook their heads in disbelief.

Turning serious, Montalvo spoke quietly, his words hitting Thornton's consciousness like .50 caliber bursts. Bo, remembering Bailey's admonition earlier, pulled his professional's mask on, putting up the shields necessary for him to carry on with the task now at hand.

"I heard on the news this morning that the PPF controls half my country, and that they are demanding recognition from the U.N. Have you heard the same, Bo?"

"Yeah, that's what Brian Gumball told me, too. What do you think will happen, Ricardo?"

Montalvo scooted back from the table, crossing his legs and pulling a Sobranie Gold from a black package in his shirt pocket. Thornton caught the acrid aroma of the tobacco as a breeze pushed a puff of it past him.

"I think time grows short for Aguilar, and for myself. If the guerrillas are successful in their bid for recognition as a legal government, there will be little use for elections. Aguilar will fight until there is nothing left to fight with, then he will bargain his way out of the country."

"Wouldn't the PPF want to have your presence in any government they formed?" asked Thornton.

"Maybe for the first year or so they are in power. After that, my voice would be too loud, my thoughts too counterrevolutionary. Remember Nicaragua, my friend. Señor Ortega read his Mao nightly in the bush. He used the moderates only as long as it took to solidify his power base in every major social and economic area of the society. Then—"

"Then he flushed them down the revolution's toilet, right?" Thornton finished for him.

"Right," concluded Montalvo.

"What makes you think Aguilar won't die in La Libertad?"

Montalvo blew a long rush of bluish smoke across the table-top. "He may, for all I know. The man is no coward. He flies combat missions against the PPF in a helicopter built especially for him. I have heard that he delights in facing death's dark eye, and that death finds favor with the colonel's performances."

"Well, this should all be over in a few days, *señor*. I can't see where there's much left to worry about," lied Thornton.

Montalvo stood, his hands on his hips as he inhaled a deep breath of fresh air from the garden's vast supply. "Ah yes, and won't that be wonderful? I am a man of the fields, Bo Thornton. It is wonderful here, the beauty and protection of the church giving us the first peace we've had in some time. But I am still a prisoner, even though my surroundings are constructed from petals and stems rather than chain and steel.

"Soon we will be able to return to our country. Hopefully, it will be the kind of country worth returning to. We are strangers here, homeless, the seed of fear always inside us. Do you know what the meaning of the word *sanctuary* is, Bo?"

Staring across the courtyard, Thornton replied he did not.

"It is the most sacred part of a church. Should one be oppressed and have no other place to go, the gift of sanctuary is available. It is a sacred asylum, a place of refuge from the storm. Without it many would perish from the hurricanes that are blowing throughout Central and South America."

"Then you are fortunate to be here," murmured Thornton, meeting Montalvo's eyes and holding them.

"Yes. I am fortunate to be here. But I am also fortunate that my family and I can count upon a man of your skills and integrity to protect our holy place of refuge. You and your men are our friends, you will always be welcome in our home when this is over." Finishing, Montalvo walked around the small table and rested both his hands lightly on Thornton's broad shoulders. "Thank you, Bo. ¡ *Muchas gracias por todo!*"

Thornton felt like shit.

CHAPTER

13

The lights of the city were magnetic, drawing his eyes to them like steel spheres. Melendez never ceased to marvel at how small the world was. Two days ago he'd been happily crawling around in the stink of other men's guts, listening to the sonic crack of bullets streaking over his head and hoping like hell that he'd see another sunrise. Now he was sitting in a cozy gringo bar, sipping fifty-year-old scotch and listening to an old Negro man skillfully playing the piano. The Guat mercenaries were in their rooms at the embassy, Melendez not trusting them to prowl the streets of San Francisco without him. Gomez, the military attaché, had rounded up a couple of sluts for the boys to play with while he was gone, a nice gesture and one he was sure would be appreciated.

They'd arrived early that evening, the chartered Lear having met them in Dallas. Colonel Gomez himself flew the group to San Francisco, giving them the sight-seer's special as they sped up the Pacific coast past Los Angeles, Monterey, and Santa Cruz. It had been an enjoyable trip.

For most of it, Melendez studied the target folder given him by Gomez. It was pleasantly accurate, complete with eight-by-eleven black-and-white photos taken by one of their embassy's local hires. The major was specifically interested in the church where Montalvo was hiding. Gomez's people had thoughtfully included a recent aerial photo as well as floor plans obtained from the city engineer's office. It gave him an exact picture of the terrain he'd have to fight in, something his military mind appreciated.

He'd been told after their arrival at the embassy that the weapons he'd asked for were being readied. Melendez wanted the basics, shotguns and magnum pistols. He didn't care what make they were, only that they were reliable and of good quality. His team would be wearing surgical gloves for the hit, allowing for the weapons to be abandoned at the scene of the attack.

He planned to take them tomorrow night, after the evening's high mass was held. In the meantime, it was time to relax. They'd provided him with a lovely young model for the evening, several thousand dollars' expense money, and an embassy limousine. His room was an expensive suite at the San Francisco Hilton, its luxury another mental shock after the wilds of eastern La Libertad.

"Another glass of wine, *señorita*?" Melendez asked the stunning redhead.

"Yes. Thank you, Major." She was just twenty-three years old, her career consisting of several magazine covers and a minor role in a made-for-television movie. Between jobs, she'd jumped at the chance to spend an evening with the man Gomez described as ". . . a wealthy Libertadian officer visiting the United States on leave from the war." She knew she'd have to bed him, but considering the gifts the major had lavished on her so far, it wouldn't be that bad a trade.

"How long will you be in San Francisco?" she asked, accepting the glass of white wine.

"A day or two," he replied, "then I must return. The war does not enjoy my being gone; she is a jealous mistress."

"I hope you'll enjoy your stay," she cooed.

Shoving his meaty hand up between her smooth legs, Melendez smiled back. "I'm sure you will do all you can to ensure my happiness and satisfction."

The girl bit her lip as the man's hard fingers burrowed into the tender flesh of her inner thigh. She hoped she'd please him, too, a feeling of dread spreading through her at the thought of what he'd do if her performance wasn't to his liking.

Bailey met Thornton on the street, the huge marble pillars of the church's entrance standing mute guard over the two men as they began talking. The sidewalks were already filling up with night people, their costumes a reflection of where their heads were at.

"Lookit all these fucking weirdos, will ya?" exclaimed Calvin, gripping the sword-cane firmly in his right hand. "Never seen so many strange motherfuckers in one city in all my life!"

A group of punkers jostled them as they passed on the sidewalk; Thornton happily twisted one of the young men's hand so that his wrist made an audible pop as Bo bent it back. "Hey! Fuck you, asshole! Come back here and try that shit again! We'll kick your fucking asses to L.A. You hear me, jerk-off?"

Their voices evaporated into the night. Thornton ignored the taunts, sure he'd broken at least one of the fragile bones in the boy's wrist.

"Yeah, I *love* this city. Reminds me of ancient Rome. All fucked up and the barbarians at the gates. How'd you like to be raising your kids here?"

Bailey jerked the cane upward, swinging it over his head, then snapping it under one arm. "I'd rather not think about that, if you don't mind. It's too depressing."

After half a block, Thornton brought up the subject of Melendez.

"The FAA notified us as soon as their Lear landed. Two DEA agents trailed them to the Libertadian embassy, two others picked up the major an hour later when he left for his hotel.

"Seems he's brought two dudes with him, passports say they're citizens, but my information says they're Guatemalans. Probably *soldados de fortuna* . . . hired guns on Melendez's payroll. They're still at the embassy, according to our boys.

"Melendez is staying at the Hilton, but is at this very minute wining and dining some redhead he picked up. Very casual, from everything we've seen so far."

Thornton steered them across the street, stopping to buy a hot dog from a corner vendor before they jumped one of the trolley cars that was rumbling down the hill. Hartung, Silver, and Bannion were escorting the Montalvos to an early movie. It wasn't the best idea, but the family was restless and so were his men. Besides, with a tail on Melendez, Thornton felt the risk was minimized. The major would assume the family was at the church, and he wasn't going to move until he was sure of his chances at success.

"Montalvo thinks everything is hunky-dory. This movie thing supports that assumption, although State would probably poop their collective diaper if they knew we were taking them out for popcorn and soda."

Bailey pulled his jacket tighter against the sudden chill. "Lippman didn't say hi. In fact, he was pretty brief this afternoon. Voice was kinda different, too."

"Shit," Thornton said softly.

Jumping from the trolley, the men quick-stepped to reach the safety of the sidewalk. Thornton was looking for a Thai restaurant he'd been told about during his last trip to Bragg. The owner had fought with Bo as a mercenary when he was with CCN. A Thai Nung, he'd survived the war and immigrated to the United States after returning to Thailand. Several former SOG officers sponsored him, providing money and a place to stay until he'd gotten on his feet.

"That's the place," Thornton said, pointing, "the Dragon's Head. Slick name, huh?"

"Gooks and their dragons . . . I just hope the food is as good as you've been telling me."

Thornton punched the former SEAL hard in the shoulder, ducking as Bailey jabbed at him with the cane. "Wan will feed you better than you've ever been fed before, squid. Plus, I want to quiz him about some of the others we left behind."

"Better you quiz him about how the hell we're gonna waste Melendez," Bailey responded.

Dinner was everything Bo promised it would be. Wan was overjoyed to see his former team leader again, both cooking and serving their meal himself. Afterward they talked, exchanging information about old friends and their fates. Before Thornton and Bailey left, Wan led them upstairs to his office, where he gave the One-Zero a battered but serviceable pump shotgun.

"I carry in Vietnam. You remember, Bo?"

"Shit yes, I remember," said Thornton, pumping the oiled action several times. Handing the shortened gun to Bailey, Thornton related several stories about Wan's expertise with the twelve-gauge during their time at CCN.

". . . then the damned dink motherfucker tried to break the ambush, and Wan here cut his legs right out from under him. We tied the stumps off with our drive-on rags, then called for extraction. The S-2 officer got what he needed before the bastard bled to death, and the Army was saved the embarrassment of having one of their firebases overrun due to the intel old Wan's shotgun provided."

Bailey handed the piece back to the Thai, who gave it again to Thornton. "I know you here doing something very dangerous, Bo. Wan can smell it on you, like the old days when we cross the rivers to kill NVA. You take Wan's gun. When finished, return it here. Wan sends his spirit with you."

Thornton shook the man's hand, stuffing the shotgun into a dark canvas bag Wan handed him. "Thanks, Wan. I'll take good care of it. The food was great, the boys at Bragg weren't lying about your cooking."

Wan grinned. "America been good to me. Easy to make money here, lots of people like Thai food in San Francisco. Hey! Where your Buddha, Bo? I no see him around your neck."

Thornton, remembering Johannson, answered, "I gave him to a friend, Wan. His luck had run out."

"Oh, I see," replied Wan. "Here, I bring several to the U.S. with me. All made by same papa-san in my village. Good magic. You give yours to friend, I give mine to friend, too."

Bo lifted the heavy ivory Buddha from Wan's open palm, its gold throne sparkling in the office's dim lighting. Squeezing it, he nodded to Wan, who smiled widely, nodding his head in return.

"Thanks, Wan. I know your Buddha will bring me much luck. We have to go now. Thank you for your kindness and hospitality; it is good to know you are alive."

"Ah, Bo-San, it is an honor for you to enter my home. I will see you when your business in San Francisco is over with. Until then, walk carefully and with both eyes open."

"That Wan character is a pretty cool little dude," Bailey offered as they strolled down the street.

"He was hell on wheels in Nam," replied Thornton. "Best damn tracker I've ever seen. And give him a bloop gun . . . oh, my Lord, what he could do with that!"

"Yeah, I never much liked the 203 myself. Too bulky all

wrapped up under an M-16. But, I knew guys who could shoot like hell with them."

They walked along in silence after that, lost in their own thoughts, the dull heat of Thai food burning like a coal oven in their bellies. Finding themselves near the Hilton, they wondered what Melendez was doing. Suddenly a burst of rifle fire broke out behind them, the rubbery squeal of tires assaulting their ears as a late-model sedan began to accelerate, gunfire raking both sides of the street as the gangbangers inside furiously pulled their triggers.

"Incoming!" yelled Bailey, throwing himself into a roll and coming up hard against the rear fender of a classic T-bird. Thornton was one car in front of him, the canvas envelope already lying empty on the sidewalk as Bo jacked a round into the shotgun's chamber.

The car was nearly even with Thornton when he blew the right front tire. As the driver lost control, Bo rolled farther down the sidewalk, jumping up to blow the windshield out with his second shot. One of the thugs, wearing a red leather jacket and black beret, leaped from the near-side passenger door, an AK-47 held one-handed. His chest sagged under the impact of Bailey's .357 hollow-points, the mushroom effect of the bullets' blowing immense hunks of bone, muscle, and flesh out the boy's back. Spinning like a top, he collapsed in the street; a taxi trying to sweep around the stalled vehicle crunched over his head as the driver raced by, blowing his horn madly.

Shotgun tucked well up into his armpit, Thornton scurried across the street, finding cover behind a mailbox as the driver's companion kicked his door open and rolled into the street. All around them people were running, diving into open doorways or lying flat on the sidewalks, some in the moist gutters. Screams, shouts, and oaths filled the air. Somewhere a siren began to whoop, joined by several more as the police responded to the flood of calls washing over the city's 911 operators.

"Motherfucker!" yelled the young man who had just exited the car. "I'll kill *all* you pig motherfuckers!" Lifting a long arm chest high, the boy pulled the trigger of a short-barreled revolver just as Thornton zeroed him with the shotgun's front sight post. A woman grabbing her belly fell forward, her head making a sodden sound as she struck the cold concrete of the sidewalk. Thornton's blast caught the gang member at waist level, driving him sideways into the car. Bo was already moving before the dead youth's body quit twitching.

"Watch the back!" warned Bailey. "We've still got two of the cocksuckers in the car!"

Thornton threw himself into a forward roll as the second backseat shooter made his dash, an Uzi submachine gun chewing up two off-duty zoo workers who'd been out window-shopping after a long day in the elephants' cage.

Lying in the middle of the street, Bo fired. The fourth shot skittered across the asphalt, slamming into the running man's ankles, literally blowing him off his feet. Bailey, running parallel to the third gunman, ducked as he heard Thornton's shotgun go off. Watching its effect, he assumed a solid kneeling position, then squeezed two shots off. The first smacked into the wounded thug's upper chest, breaking his shoulder as it plowed through tissue and bone, ripping blood vessels apart and shattering muscle as though it were hard plastic. The second meat mutilator crashed into the dying man's chin, blowing his lower jaw away, teeth and facial features exploding in a high-pressure mist that covered the now-still body.

"Freeze! You make one silly fucking move and I'll blow this bitch's eyes outta her wop head!"

The speaker, a tough-looking black youth of about nineteen, stood out on the sidewalk holding a wicked-looking Desert Eagle .357 automatic. The deep blue of the slide glinted dangerously in the street's overhead lighting, its barrel pressed hard against a middle-aged woman who looked ready to die without any help from her captor. Police units were now blocking both ends of the street, the officers yanking shotguns from their cars, and moving slowly up along the still-lit store fronts. Hearing the man's threat, they froze, uncertain of what they should do next.

Thornton knew. He knew this young punk would never let the woman go. He might drag her down the street and into an alley, where he'd blow her brains out. Or he might demand a car from someone, then drive her a few blocks away before turning off her lights for good. In any event, someone was going to die, and Thornton's vote was already cast in favor of Mr. Billy T. Badass.

Picking himself up from the street, Bo raised the shotgun to his shoulder and began a slow walk toward the hostage taker. Bailey, on the other side of the odd couple, held his position. Raising his Magnum and taking careful aim, he willed his thoughts to draw the gunman's attention toward himself as Bo slipped closer. Seeing Bailey, the last remaining gangbanger jerked the woman closer, whispering loudly into her ear.

"Hey, girl, lookee here. This *bad* motherfucker with a gun don't believe ole Linel won't keep his word to blow your ass away. Well, I'm gonna do just that if he don't drop that little toy of his . . . and I mean right damned now!" To emphasize his point, the man now known as Linel pushed the heavy Magnum's barrel downward and pulled the trigger, the bullet splitting the woman's foot, causing her to sag against the smiling black man in a near faint.

"Yo, junior! Why don't you just let the lady go, and me and my partner will kill your ugly ass faster than you can peel a Chiquita-fucking-banana."

Linel's head spun. Seeing the pump gun's dark orifice staring at him, he nearly dropped his own weapon recovering only because he realized the big bastard holding it couldn't pull the trigger. "You stupid jive-ass honky piece of whale shit. No fuckin' way you gonna blow me down with that cannon! That bad boy would take me and the bitch to hell together. Best you back off now, and let me move it on down the street."

Bailey pulled his trigger. The 158-grain slug covered the fifteen feet between him and the black in less than a second. It struck him high on the only fully exposed portion of his head, the non-fatal wound stunning the man, causing him to lose his hold on the woman, who slumped to the sidewalk without a sound.

Thornton sidestepped to take himself out of the line of fire, then sent a solid hail of buckshot into Linel's upper torso. The concentrated force of the blast pushed the man several feet closer to Bailey, who was now lying prone on the sidewalk, well out of Thornton's spread. Pumping the Model 19's trigger twice, Calvin sent two bladder busters spinning into the screaming black's lower belly.

Watching the body fall to the hard cement, Thornton leaped forward, jacking his last round into the breech. Coming to a halt mere feet from the nearly dead man's figure, Bo dropped the sawed-off blaster to hip level and pulled the trigger one final time. The lead shot peeled nearly two feet of skin up from the corpse's chest, dragging bits of white bone and gristle along behind. Still-burning powder ignited Linel's shirt, wisps of smoke curling skyward.

Only the echo of gunfire was left as the gunman rasped out his last breath, its putrid smell gagging the two men standing over his trashed body.

"Uh, you guys *are* cops, aren't you?"

Bailey looked up to see who the speaker was. "That's correct, Officer. I'm Special Agent Bailey, DEA. This is Agent Kilgore. You want to secure this area while I radio my people?"

The young police officer lowered his revolver, a look of relief swimming across his face. "Sure, anything you say. You can use my car's mobile, it's the one nearest the corner. Shit, I'm glad you guys wasted these pukes, the paper work's gonna be *murder!*"

Pushing through the crowd, Thornton and Bailey headed back the way they'd come. Bo reached down, jerking Wan's cloth guncase from the sidewalk where it had fallen. Stuffing the still-hot weapon into its maw, he whistled a long sigh of relief.

"You notice every time we go out to eat in this town, we end up killing at least four people we've never even met before?"

Pointing out Bailey's cane in the hands of another officer, Thornton waited while Bailey flashed his tin and collected the sword. "Yeah," he said as the DEA man rejoined him, "makes you want to order in, doesn't it?"

Calvin snorted as he noted the long tear in his new slacks. "We'd better get back to Delgado's; I'll head in to the office. This is gonna take the rest of the night to put to bed. No need for you to be involved any more than you are."

They flagged a taxi down, ordering the Oriental driver to drop them a half-block from the church. Sitting together in the backseat, neither man spoke until they were nearly to Bo's destination.

"What kind of fool drives a car down a crowded street shooting at people?" Thornton asked himself. "When that kinda shit happened in Vietnam, we called it terrorism. When the VC who were responsible were caught, they were executed on the spot. These punks aren't even animals, they're a lower life-form, one that we need to eradicate like a deadly virus."

The cab pulled to the curb, Thornton hopping out and looking down through Bailey's open window. "I'll see you in the morning?"

Calvin grinned back. "Not unless I see you first."

With that, the driver spurted back into the night's traffic, leaving Thornton alone with Wan's shotgun, the smell of burnt gunpowder hanging heavy in the air.

CHAPTER
14

The president's office was a lavish affair. Aguilar preferred it that way, a symbol of his absolute power and authority. It was in this office that he was now sitting, one of three phones in his hand. Azo stood quietly off to one side as Gomez briefed the president. Outside, the sound of distant explosions grumbled across the capital's rooftops. The guerrillas, emboldened by their successful ambush of Quevar's battalion, were sending in small units to disrupt power and communication lines. The Army was doing its best, but it couldn't be everywhere at once.

"Do the Americans know Melendez is in the city?" asked Aguilar.

The scratchy sound of Gomez's voice skipped across the line, a constant buzz threatening to make it unintelligible. "Yes, *mi Presidente*. I did as you commanded, putting him up in a downtown hotel, a large amount of spending money, a woman who attracts attention just by stepping outdoors. They know he's here, of that I'm sure."

Aguilar spun in his chair so that he could look out over the city. La Libertad was beautiful, he reminded himself. The hollow grunt of an explosion disturbed his train of thought. "Gomez? Are you there?"

"*Si, mi Presidente*. I can hear you."

"These damned phones! No wonder we have such problems, we can't even communicate with each other!" Aguilar motioned for Azo to bring him a cigar from the box near the door. After clipping it, he lit the long brown tube of tobacco, resuming his conversation with the military attaché.

113

"I am sending Azo along with two other Wolves. They will arrive late tonight in Los Angeles. Have them driven to San Francisco. Provide them what they ask for, and keep them away from Melendez and his people."

Gomez, alone in his office, looked at the phone with a perplexed expression on his handsome face. "*Presidente*, a *second* team? By why? Melendez is sure he can do the job, he plans to go after Montalvo tomorrow night."

Aguilar blew a thick funnel of smoke out the open window. Gomez was one of his better officers, although he was more suited to dinner parties and other men's wives than ground combat. That was why he was sent to the United States, his kind had their purpose in diplomatic circles. "*Mi Colonel*, the gringos know we are going to have to try and kill Ricardo. I believe they planned his fortunate 'escape,' and even now they are guarding him with Delgado's help.

"We know they debriefed Montalvo. Therefore, we know *they* know who Melendez is. I have given them what they want most, a recognizable target. While they are expending their forces chasing the major, Azo will be hunting our prey.

"Do you now understand, Colonel Gomez?"

"Yes, *Presidente*. But what if Melendez strikes first . . . and succeeds?"

Aguilar laughed harshly. "That would be like Melendez, and should it happen, Azo's instructions are to kill the major and any surviving members of the team.

"In fact, Major Melendez will die regardless of how Montalvo meets his fate. We will claim to have discovered the major's plot to assassinate Montalvo, and that we sent our own people to intercept him if possible.

"I have already erased any record of his leave orders, and his apartment has been 'salted' with incriminating evidence as to his secret ties to the PPF.

"As with any political killing, Gomez, one has to have a scapegoat. Major Luis Melendez is our goat, and you will ensure he fulfills his role. ¿*Entende?*"

Gomez nodded into the phone. "Yes, yes I understand. You can inform your people we will be waiting for them. There is an apartment we keep for just such 'visits'; they can stay there. I personally will inform them of the major's plans."

"Good!" exclaimed Aguilar. "With any good fortune at all we will see Montalvo dead within forty-eight hours. Should the major fail, Azo's group will carry on with the mission. I want them covered should anything go wrong. Is that understood?"

Nodding his head at the affirmative reply from the other end, Aguilar gave the colonel his best and hung up. Placing the half-smoked stogie on the lip of his desk, he turned to the lean Salvadoran and spoke. "You heard?"

A nod.

"Do not underestimate Melendez. He may succeed. If he does, you will have to kill him in the embassy. If he should fail, you must ensure Montalvo's death as well as the major's.

"At the same time I wouldn't mind seeing the priest dead, too. If it can be arranged, you will find a healthy deposit in your account."

The mercenary nodded again.

Aguilar stood, reaching for the pistol belt hanging from the back of his chair. "In any event, kill Gomez before you return. His knowledge of this matter is necessary, but his continued existence is not, once our work is finished. I can replace my peacocks."

Azo's expression never changed. He only nodded a third time, then waited for Aguilar to call for his car. They were attending the funeral of Colonel Quevar, whose body had been returned to the capital for burial.

The Salvadoran appreciated the irony of his mission. First he would bury a colonel, then he would kill one. He didn't question his assignments, he simply carried them out. Once he had joined a group of guerrillas for an entire month. During that time he won their respect, shooting and killing many of the president's own soldiers in ambushes and night attacks.

At the end of the month, he'd turned an M-60 machine gun on the band as they slept. He'd brought out much intelligence on the PPF's movements and plans. Aguilar's compensation for his success had been generous.

War, to Azo, was a question of invincibilities and vulnerabilities. So far he'd proven to be invincible, but that could change with the careless snap of a twig during a midnight stalk. He would be careful in San Francisco, he would be invincible.

"The car is here, Azo. Let's not be late for Quevar's final parade."

As Aguilar strode by him, the grim-faced Salvo merely nodded, then followed the president down the marble stairs leading to the sweeping drive out front.

CHAPTER
15

Hartung slipped the door to the small kitchen open, closing it soundlessly behind him as he entered the dimly lit room. As he did so, Bannion, pouring himself a cup of coffee from the pot near the stove, turned and nodded a silent greeting. It was quiet throughout the house, the kind of stillness that encourages a deep and fitful sleep.

"Pretty chilly out."

"Airborne and amen," replied the sergeant major.

Bannion dipped a spoon into the half-full sugar cup, dropping its sweet load into his cup. "Anything unusual tonight?"

Hartung slipped his subgun's sling over his head, laying the stubby black weapon carefully on the table. Unzipping the dark blue down jacket he was wearing, Frank pulled one of the simple wooden breakfast chairs out and sat down. The dive watch he wore confirmed it was past 0200. "Nope," he casually drawled, "lots of traffic, a few stray cats running the fence. Other than that, it's as quiet as a tomb."

"Coffee?"

"Please."

Bannion lifted a second cup from the nearby tray and poured it full of the strong black liquid. Lifting both his and the sergeant major's, he padded across the tiled floor in rubber-soled SWAT boots, quiet as a cat himself. Handing Frank the cup, Bannion took an exploratory sip from his own. "I guess I pull until oh five hundred, then Jason comes on, right?"

Hartung grunted, savoring the steaming swirl of his drink as it cascaded down the back of this throat. "Yeah. What'd you think of tonight's high mass?"

The sturdy SLAM operative paused in his function check of his MAC-11. The gun was a favorite, with thirty-two .380 tummy ticklers per magazine, and muzzled with a Sionics suppressor so that all one heard when it was in action was the slappity-slap of the bolt punching lead down the tube.

Satisfied, he slipped the now-loaded weapon into its black nylon holster. Adjusting the dual leg straps so they weren't quite as tight, Mike then checked the four magazine pouches riding securely on his left upper hip. The rig had been specially built by John Carver, a magician when it came to high-speed/low-drag special-ops gear. Along with the holster and mag holders, Bannion carried a long-bladed K-Bar combat knife, a small folder, flashlight, and first-aid kit. The entire unit rode snugly around his waist, a two-inch-wide cordura belt fastened by a quick-release Zytel buckle supporting the entire kit.

"Where'd you get that fancy rig, Mike?"

"DEA issues these to us, every one is custom fit to the agent. I like this little MAC, so the holster needed to be dialed in especially for the gun. It's a slick deal; GSG-9 and GIGN have similar setups."

Hartung recognized the two units Bannion mentioned as being premier antiterrorists outfits; one German, the other French. "Well, give me a comfortable set of LBE any day. It served this old man for thirty years, and I'll bet ya it'll be around for thirty more."

They both laughed, knowing there was no such thing as a "comfortable" load-bearing harness.

Grabbing a black DEA baseball cap he'd conned Bailey out of, Bannion slipped it onto his head, adjusting the brim so it rode high and casual. In his heavy wool fisherman's sweater and black Levis he looked like Hollywood's version of the ultimate warrior. "Didn't you ask me something about mass tonight?"

Frank leaned back in his chair, beginning to unwind from his shift on guard. "Yeah, I did. You get any feelings from it?"

Bannion fixed the rugged shadow warrior with a thoughtful stare before answering. "Matter of fact, I did. Seemed like someone was watching us, I mean really *watching* everything we did.

Kinda stupid, I mean, the church was filled with people and all . . ."

"But you still felt bugs running up and down your spine, right?"

Mike nodded.

"Me, too. This Melendez boy is out there looking us over, that I'm sure of. Either he or one of his pets was in that church tonight, maybe all damned three of the bastards. What we got was a visual recon, although it wouldn't have been a bad place to try a hit, when you think about it."

"So why didn't he?" countered Bannion.

"Who knows except Melendez? Too many people in the way, bad angle on the family, or perhaps the major just plain got weird vibes from the mass itself.

"Remember what Bo told us. This guy's a pro, trained by our government and two or three others. He'll pick the time and place, and he'll pick it soon. He's got to have a confirmed kill so the action will be tongue-touching close. Makes me wish Lee was here; we could use another good man."

At the mention of David Lee's name, Bannion recalled Thornton's telling him about the Special Forces sergeant he'd replaced. "Lee sounds like a stud, a regular part of your band of merry men?"

Hartung's face crumbled into a smile. "Yeah, Dave's a bad motherfucker. He and Bo were on the same A-team in Panama when Bo retired. From what I hear, Lee picked up A-13 as team daddy after getting outta the hospital recently. Good man, wasn't in Nam but he's done his share of shit for good old Uncle Sam."

Bannion acknowledged Frank's assessment of Lee with a smile, then headed for the door. "See you later in the morning, Sergeant Major. Get some Z's."

"You got it, Mike. Good hunting." After the burly former SEAL slipped into the night's gloom, Frank considered having another cup of coffee, then decided to pass. He was impressed with the big blond's performance, happy that he was as professional as his file made him out to be. Sure and steady, easy to get along with, but not overly friendly. Bailey, the little runt, had provided them a fitting substitute for Lee.

Policing up both their mugs, Hartung snatched his micro Uzi

from the table and prepared to head for his room. Stopping at the sink to wash out the cups, he was again overwhelmed by a sense of uneasiness. It was the same feeling he'd had when Muc Hoq got overrun by the NVA in '69. He'd experienced the premonitions several more times, and hadn't been wrong once. Those had been recon teams, though; teams whose missions went to hell as soon as they'd left the deck of the unmarked helicopters dropping them deep into enemy territory. The worst had been RT Arctic, inserting for the first time to conduct a bomb-damage assessment for the Air Force.

The entire team was butchered while Frank and some of the others on stand-down listened helplessly to the RTO calling the plays over the team's PRC-77. As he recalled, Daniels, the team's newly promoted One-Zero, had agreed to let the RTO straphang on the mission. Payjack was on his way home after a second tour with CCN, his orders sending him back to the World the following week. He volunteered for the mission, knowing the new cherry wasn't yet comfortable with the radio procedure CCN used. "I'll just be helping Daniels out, Frank. His RTO is a bit hinky still, and having an extra American along might chill him out."

Frank remembered urging the seasoned jungle fighter not to go. Straphangers, especially those who were one-digit midgets, seemed to attract bullets. Hartung didn't want to see that happen to Payjack.

The Spike team found them in a broken wagon-wheel perimeter atop the small hill where they'd stood to fight. The ground for fifty meters around was littered with the flotsam of battle. Splintered rifle butts gave evidence to the fierceness of hand-to-hand combat. Spent brass lay in small piles where the defenders had lain, each circle of brass indicating how the perimeter had shrunk with each NVA assault. The choking smell of cordite intermingled with the aroma of the turned earth, a sharp tang of burnt bodies giving the air a faintly exotic odor. The bodies reflected the fight's ferocity by their wounds. Many of the NVA had been chewed apart by Cobra gunships, their corpses often missing entire body parts because of the intense fire.

Others, the ones farther down the hill and in the treeline, were shrapnel-filled sponges. One-oh-five fire from the grunt unit that supported them came in "danger close" on Paycheck's command. In between the two extremes, the NVA had been pummeled by claymores and grenades, along with round after round of .223 fire provided by the team's stubby black Colt Commandos. It was Payjack who'd stayed on the Prick 77, calling in the various support fires until the enemy was too close for even SOG's comfort. Hartung squeezed his eyes shut, recalling the distant echo of small-arms fire seeping into Payjack's handset while the man gave the TOC a running account of what was happening.

It ended when the sound of bugles joined the din, Payjack commenting dryly that the bad guys were rushing the quarterback. His voice was unnaturally clear in the stuffy tent, coating them all with dread as the box speaker broadcast the team's final minutes. "Here they come!" Payjack barked . . . a burst from a CAR-15, then two more interrupting his commentary. "Here they fucking come . . . all over us . . . Daniels is down hard, so's the last 'Yard. . . . Shit, they're bayoneting the poor bastards . . . no one left, Frank . . . no one but me. . . ." A long barrel-melting burst of gunfire, then silence so profound that the men in the tent began yelling at the speaker, hoping against hope that the RTO could somehow have survived the conflagration around him. All they heard was a dark, heavy silence, then the handset was keyed again, Payjack's last words branding them with their finality. "Frank? They're here, they're—"

Hartung himself flew in with the Spike team. He was the first man to reach the body-infested hilltop. They'd been NVA, all right. Cream-of-the-crop headhunters straight from Uncle Ho's personal garden. The team had slaughtered over a hundred of them, using guns, grenades, claymores, arty, air support, and finally, bare knuckles and knives. Frank found Payjack's body propped up against the shattered squad radio, a single bullet hole in his forehead. He'd been alive when the NVA had finally overrun the position. Wounded yes, but alive.

They'd executed him where he sat, the handset clutched in his bandaged hand, blood forming a thin crust between the damaged fingers. Hartung wanted to scream, to cry, to strike out against the murderous slime who'd blown away his friend with no more thought than how close he could stand without getting spattered by the 7.62 × 39mm's frightful impact.

Bodies loaded, they'd returned to the launch site only to discover the REMFs, upon hearing the news about the team's annihilation, had broken into the dead men's hooches and stolen everything of value, including the unissued team patches Daniels kept in his footlocker. The Soggers had kicked ass after seeing that shit, dragging the hapless administrative pukes out of their tents and offices, shoving carbines and captured Tokarevs into their faces and threatening to kill the lot of them unless the gear was returned.

It was, but the teams extracted a heavy toll from every man who'd taken part in the looting, sending a select handful to the hospital in Saigon with major injuries from the beatings administered.

Standing over the sink, cup in hand, Frank remembered it all. He had the same gut-knotting awareness of something about to happen now. Turning to climb the stairs, he decided to wake Thornton. You had to trust your hunches, he reminded himself. Bo would understand his concern and do something about it. There were times that gut feelings were the best intel source you could have, and Frank knew from experience this was one of those times.

Coming to his friend's darkened room, Hartung tapped lightly on the slightly open door. "Bo? It's me, Frank...."

The soft sound of steel being drawn across a leather belt reached his ears. "Come on in, Frank. I feel it, too...."

They'd left their car several blocks from the church, walking along the city's sidewalks like men who'd just come off the night shift at some factory: tired, hungry, thinking only of bed. They attracted no attention to themselves, blending in with the thin crowd still out on the street even at this early hour. Reaching the high wall that separated the church's grounds from the rest of the city, Melendez stopped to light a cigarette. Sharing it, the three waited until the *calle* was clear, then boosted the lightest of the two Guatemalans up so that he was sitting atop the thick adobe barrier.

Slipping a small yet sturdy grappling hook from under his

coat, the merc carefully placed one of the rubber-coated spikes so that it formed an anchor for his companions. Uncoiling the short climbing rope, he dropped it to Melendez, who joined him in an instant. Seconds later the last man was on the wall, thick knots tied in the rope giving him sure footing as he scaled the obstacle.

On hands and knees they moved, a thick overhang of coastal pine their objective. Upon reaching it, Melendez signaled a halt. They were directly behind the house Montalvo was holed up in. All that stood between them and their target was the expansive backyard, itself littered with lawn furniture and tastefully landscaped shrubbery.

Touching each of the legionnaires on the shoulder, Melendez silently ordered them to check their equipment. They were all armed with compact riot shotguns and .44 caliber Magnum revolvers. In addition, each man carried three fragmentation grenades and a combat knife of his choosing. They were, he thought, loaded for bear.

After the Guats signaled their readiness, Melendez reversed the grappling hook so that they could now climb down and into the walled enclosure. He himself would cover their infiltration from the wall's ledge. Once they were securely in place, he would proceed farther down the narrow track until reaching another wall which intersected it. This would take him past a small shed used to store gardening equipment. The tiled roof of the outbuilding was built up against the wall itself, and would allow him to traverse from the walkway to the main house. According to the floorplans he'd studied, there was a small balcony which led directly into what he supposed was the upstairs library.

It would be at this point that he'd effect his entrance.

The Guatemalans' job was quite simple. They were to seek out whoever was on guard, and neutralize him. Afterward they would throw their grenades into the lower portion of the building, and engage the occupants who attempted to either confront them or flee. Melendez knew they couldn't cover the front, but he planned on a lightning-quick raid which would catch his enemy off guard.

Once the assault was under way, Melendez would enter by means of the balcony and find the Montalvos. The schematic showed the bedrooms to be on the second floor, so all he needed do was shoot anyone leaving a room. His men had been ordered not to climb the stairs so that they wouldn't chance coming under their leader's deadly fire. There would be enough confusion as it was.

A locked door would mean he'd found his quarry. A kick, a grenade, then a few well-placed rounds from his alley sweeper would finish the job. They'd rally back at the wall because the police units, he knew, would be responding upon the first sounds of gunfire being reported. From that point on it would be a race between the authorities and himself for the sanctuary of the Libertadian embassy.

Bannion stood in the far corner of the yard, the apex of the two walls providing him a niche where he could listen to the night's sounds. Hartung had clicked the kitchen's light off a half hour before, leaving the house in near-total darkness. Only a single table lamp burned in the large living room at his end of the villa. Silver had taken to sleeping on the couch, maintaining that his odd hours would disturb those upstairs. This way they would have an armed presence on the main floor, with two others upstairs. The outdoor man would cover the rear, leaving the police and Delgado's private security service with responsibility for the front.

Not even a "puddy tat" out now, the seasoned special-ops agent reflected. It had been five minutes since he'd heard a car rush down the street hidden by the massive wall behind him. If it continued like this for the rest of his shift, he'd be happy.

The unnatural silence crept up on him like a thief. His combat antenna was already sending signals to the rest of his body before he was fully aware of the danger lurking somewhere in the yard. Softly sinking into the manicured ground, Bannion cocked his head first one way, then the other. After several seconds his ear caught the sound of someone, or something, scuffing the surface of the fence on his side. He felt his breathing quicken as the adrenaline began to squirt into his system. Melendez was here; he knew it, felt it. It *could* be your average midnight rambler looking for a quick score on some household goodies. But Bannion doubted it.

Easing the MAC from its holster, Mike lowered himself to the earth until he was lying flat. He knew the intruder would be searching for him, but like most people, he'd problaby ignore ground level, preferring to scan directly in front and above him. Bannion could also use the concentration of light that gathered at his level, the dew bouncing moonbeams skyward in combination with the city's electric glow from the cloud cover coming off the bay.

It was Thornton's idea to issue them all a silver police whistle. At any sign of trouble they were to blow it, alerting everyone that danger was close by. Bannion's hung around his neck, tucked between his sweater and the ballistic vest he had on underneath. Should he use it now, or wait until he'd confirmed the intruder? Choosing to wait, the man from SLAM began inching down the length of the secondary wall. If he could get back on to the stone veranda, there was a chance he could alert Silver inside. In any event, Bannion needed to get closer to the house. Should the phantom rush the place, he'd need a better field of fire. From where Mike was now, it would be impossible to track a moving target for longer than a few short seconds.

Suddenly he froze. A brief flicker of movement emerged from the opposite corner. He could barely make out the figure of a man kneeling next to a hedge of red roses. Drawing the MAC across the wet grass so that its petite muzzle lined up on the shadow, he slipped the whistle from its warm berth with his other hand.

It looked like his decisions were about to be made for him.

Melendez watched as they dropped like great black spiders to the soft ground below. They'd seen no sign of a guard, although there was a soft light coming from one of the rooms at the far end of the house. Giving his men a few moments of extra cover, he began his trek toward the gardener's shed. He had expected to find splinters of fractured glass strewn along the passageway, but was relieved to discover none. Careless, he thought. Perhaps they were using motion detectors or ground sensors instead of the traditional anti-intrusion devices? Well, he'd soon find out.

It took him half the time he'd expected to reach his first objective. Gingerly feeling the condition of the tiles nearest him, Melendez decided they were good enough to trust his weight to. Carefully crossing over from the wall to the shed, he slithered on his belly until he reached the metal gutter that ringed the tiny structure. He would wait here, the dark cavity of the balcony beckoning him to enter, its wrought-iron railing looking like spiked teeth in the moon's subtle glow.

Soon, he whispered to himself. Soon enough I will have restored my honor and accomplished my duty. Resting his stubbled chin atop his hands, Melendez rehearsed the next few minutes in his mind. This was a technique he'd perfected in jump school. From the moment he entered the aircraft he began going over every step required to exit it. Melendez played the entire jump sequence through his mind's eye, from the twenty minute warning onward. By the time he was standing in the door, 1850 feet above the ground, he *knew* how the jump would go. The rest of the exercise was elementary, a momentary thrill which always had a happy ending.

In his mind's eye tonight, he watched himself blowing Ricardo Montalvo's cheesy little Communist head clear off his shoulders. The image brought a wry grin to his shadowed face.

Silver, lying on the couch, put the book he was reading down on the coffee table. Checking his watch, he wondered where Bannion was. Normally the guy stopped at the huge window facing the backyard and tapped him a hello on one of the thick glass panes. Jason's habit of staying up late to read often kept him awake until the wee hours of the morning, devouring books on a multitude of subjects.

The one he was just finishing had to do with a covert team of former special-operations personnel. It was one of a series, and Jason thought it entertaining. Not that shit like the author wrote about could ever be more than fiction, Silver thought. After all, Jason was part of the real thing, and *nothing* as weird as what this guy dreamed up ever happened to him.

Deciding to get a quick glass of water before turning in, the explosives expert grabbed his Glock 17 9mm off the floor, where he'd set it before lying down. Slipping the automatic behind his belt, he took several steps toward the kitchen before remembering the compact CAR-15. Never can tell, he mused aloud. Snagging the lightweight assault rifle from its corner, he checked the magazine and chamber, then, satisfied it was combat ready, headed for the darkened kitchen.

Outside, Bannion watched Silver disappear from the living room, rifle in his hand. Shit! he thought to himself. Don't come looking for me, Jason. You open that door now and this joker's going to blow you away for sure. Squinting, Bannion could make out a second figure slightly behind the first. Deciding to engage, the covert commando drew a careful bead between the two men, planning to sweep right then left as the subgun barked out its load of 85-grain subsonic rounds. With any luck at all he'd nail at least one of the jitbags, maybe wound the other bad enough to render him ineffective.

The weapon's sear was beginning to slip when Bannion caught the glimmer of a light coming on in the kitchen. Seconds later the door swung open, Jason stepping into the frame, fully outlined like a cutout doll. "Hey, Mike! Where the hell are you, pal?"

Silver's voice carried easily across the grounds, resounding in Mike's ears like one long echo. Scratch Plan A, hello, Plan B, he ruminated. Dragging in a double lungful of air, Bannion blew with all his might into the whistle clenched between his teeth. A ghoulish shriek split the night's deadly calm, startling even the man whose weapon was now chattering silently in his tight fist.

"What the fuck!" yelled Silver, throwing himself backward onto the kitchen floor as the shrill scream of Bannion's signal ricocheted off the windows. A millisecond later, he heard the unmistakable resonation of a shotgun going off, the sound followed by the crashing of glass and silverware where the double-aught steel balls impacted above him. "Holy Mother of God," he muttered, "if you want to be by yourself Mike, there's other ways of letting me know!"

Silver jerked his own whistle from a pocket, blowing loudly while he scrambled out of the kitchen and into the hallway. Upstairs he could hear the sound of feet running, then doors opening. A woman's high-pitched voice floated down the stairwell; Mrs. Montalvo he figured. Then it was quiet again.

Bannion emptied the magazine knowing full well he'd missed his targets. They'd begun moving as soon as the alarm was sounded, gliding out of his line of fire like ghosts. Ejecting the clip from its well, he effortlessly reloaded a second, then, with a quick glance right and left, leaped to his feet and began running. There was a side door which would give him entrance to the living room, from there he could support Silver downstairs while Hartung and Bo dealt with any threat coming from the house's second level.

It was only then that Bannion remembered Bo's warning that *three* hitters were to be expected. Where the fuck was the third?

The Latinos moved instantly on hearing the whistle's earsplitting blast. As they did so, a long section of grass exploded behind them, several rounds catching the larger of the two Guats just behind his calf. They barely broke the skin, but the pain urged him forward in the wake of his companion's trail. They both unleashed a volley at the man in the doorway, unsure if they'd managed to hit him. Slipping a baseball grenade from the small bag around his neck, the first mercenary, known as Crazy Horse, signaled his partner to blow the living-room window out of its frame.

Swearing at the wet sensation running down his lower leg, the second merc took careful aim and proceeded to empty the ornate framework of its eighteenth-century glass. Before the last reverberation of gunfire ceased, Crazy Horse sidearmed the frag through the shattered window. Not having to worry about it bouncing back, he threw with full force, not wanting to give anyone inside the opportunity of returning the favor.

Then both freebooters began running for the empty kitchen.

Mike ran parallel to the cool wall, coming to a stop just before reaching the small double doors leading into the living room. Risking a blast from Silver's CAR, he rapped loudly on one of the carefully fitted panes, then whispered Jason's name. Receiving no response, Bannion knelt down and opened the door. Encouraged that the room didn't erupt into gunfire, he slipped inside, staying low and moving fast.

The deadly downpour of spinning glass from the picture window's destruction drove the agent to the floor. Bannion sensed something flying through the air above him before realizing what it was. The dull thump of the grenade landing feet away from him was an all-too-familiar sound. Rolling madly, he managed to put the couch Silver slept on between himself and the lethal ball before it exploded in flame and hot spinning metal.

The force of the blast lifted the heavy couch from the floor, dropping it squarely on top of the stunned man's back. A steel roller struck him soundly at the base of the skull, opening a deep wound, which began bleeding profusely. Bannion's last thought before passing out was of Jason's book, now lying ripped and torn on the floor before him. The cover pictured a lean commando leaping out of a ball of bright orange fire. The words above the scowling face read *The Night Raider*, and for the briefest of moments Bannion thought the man looked strangely like the FBI agent he'd clobbered at the hotel.

Then the world around him turned a deep black as he spun into unconsciousness.

In the aftermath of the blast, Silver steadied his carbine's barrel against the heavy oak banister. Moments later the first figure burst through the still-open door leading into the backyard. Jason waited an extra second, then fired a burst of three. His intuition was rewarded when they caught the second shadow as he popped into view. The Latin raider dropped to his knees as if he'd been struck by an ax. Skidding across the tiles for several more feet, he stopped just short of the second doorway, then fell forward so that his head was within arm's reach of the ex-Ranger.

Not wanting to take any chances, Jason reached behind his back and grabbed a heavy-bladed combat throwing knife. Slipping forward, careful to remain out of the first interloper's line of sight, Silver raised the double-edged blade above his head, then brought it sharply down against the dead man's upper vertebra. The knife cut through the bone and attaching cartilage as if it were thick cheese, a wash of blood flowing onto the floor and around Jason's knees as he freed the blade from its human sheath.

"One down and one to go," the wiry blade master chortled to himself. Then he was moving, wondering momentarily where Bannion might be.

Thornton rolled off his bed onto the floor. He had just faintly heard the whistle, relying primarily on the two rapid shotgun blasts to alert him that the hit was on. After Frank's visit he had continued stropping the Russian springblade until the hairs seemed to leap from his arm before the edge touched them. Loading the custom-crafted Crain blade into the knife's handle, Bo set the safety, then shoved the mechanism deftly into the belt sheath he'd brought along with his other gear.

Before lying down to rest, he checked both the shotgun and 645, ensuring they were locked and loaded. Thornton, like Hartung, would be staying in his clothes for the rest of the night. He respected the sergeant major's gut instinct, Bo'd had a few of those himself in times past. Slipping the end of the gold chain he wore through Wan's smiling Buddha, he snapped the necklace closed, then rubbed the ivory figure's belly with his thumb and forefinger. For luck, he thought quietly to himself, we're gonna need it.

Frank was already in the hallway, knocking rapidly on Maritza's door when Thornton rushed out of his room. They both turned toward the top of the stairs when the Guatemalan blew the living-room window out, involuntarily dropping into semi-crouches as the grenade exploded downstairs. Seconds later Silver's short burst told them he was still alive, leaving Bo free to get to Montalvo.

While Hartung urged the frightened girl to wrap a robe around herself and follow him down the hall, Thornton spoke quickly with Ricardo. "Frank'll be in here with you and the family," he said calmly. "Once the door is shut, do exactly what he says to. The police are on their way right now. All we have to do is hold Melendez off for a few more minutes, and it'll be all over."

Slipping the stainless-steel automatic from his belt, Bo handed it to the smaller man. "You know how to use one of these?" he asked. Ricardo nodded briskly.

"Good. It's got a round in the chamber, nine more in the magazine. Just aim and pull the trigger. You've already killed a man, so the hardest part now is going to be hitting your target."

Frank pushed past the two men and into the spacious bedroom. Even freshly pulled from her bed Maritza was beautiful, although she was shaking as she went to her mother. "You better get out there, Bo. I'll secure us here."

Thornton noted that Frank was fully dressed, his weapon hanging from its sling around his neck. A Browning Hi-Power was in his hand, the standard magazine replaced with a twenty-one-rounder which protruded a full inch from the magazine well.

"Roger that, Frank. See you in a few."

"Airborne and amen!" replied Hartung, then the door was closed.

As Thornton turned he caught a brief glimpse of someone stepping back into the shadows at the opposite end of the hall. Knowing none of the team was upstairs, he dropped the shotgun's barrel from where it lay against his shoulder and fired at where the apparition had appeared. The deep boom of a heavy Magnum caused him to drop to the floor as the bullet ripped a deep-seated gouge in the door he'd been standing in front of. Jacking another fat shell into the weapon's breech, Thornton knew who he was facing.

Major Luis Adolfo Garcia Melendez.

Jason Silver crouched in the entranceway, his carbine pointed so that he could cover both the long passageway leading to the kitchen as well as the entrance to the living room on his left. He could easily see the decapitated remains of the man he'd just killed lying in the kitchen door, a wide pool of blood growing still larger as the body drained itself. The mercenary's head sat like a lone island in the middle of the crimson pond, glassy eyes wide open, its tongue hanging from between split lips like a sprung drawbridge.

He felt the rush of the man as the distance between them evaporated. Glimpsing only a shadow, Jason managed to bring the rifle up so that he was able to lever the charging figure over his head, flipping the Guat into the hall between himself and the front door. Dropping the barrel to waist level, he flinched as Bo's shotgun went off upstairs, then shuddered as he heard the soft *ping* of the grenade's handle as it flew free from the frag's round body. Letting go of the Colt, he threw himself into the shattered living room, curling into a ball as the concussion rolled over him.

Feeling for the Glock, he realized he'd lost it, choosing then to pull the Moeller Viper from its sheath. The knife had barely cleared leather when the remaining mercenary stepped cautiously into the room. From outside, the two men could hear the wail of sirens as police units from all over the city began to converge on the church. Three cars were already in place, their bright emergency lights bathing the living room in shades of red and blue as the mirrored reflectors spun madly inside their plastic housings.

"You are one ugly dick licker, aren't you?" hissed Silver. "Your mama have any kids that lived?" he said in Spanish. The man smiled wickedly, shaking his head no.

"Oh, oh," Jason said to himself. "This bastard's already dead. Mrs. Silver's boy better not screw this one up or he's gonna be in a world of hurt."

The Guat, seeing the sparkle of Jason's knife in the weirdly swirling lights, grinned even wider. Gently setting his shotgun down, the mercenary pulled a short machete from the sheath hanging down his back. Its edge had been laboriously hand honed for hours until it could cut a silk handkerchief in the air. Silver recognized the weapon immediately and began to sweat. He'd seen what a machete could do in unskilled hands, but the damage it could do wielded by *this* motherfucker left his mouth dry.

The two men began to close the distance between each other. Silver slid one foot, then another across the floor. His knees were slightly bent, body weight squarely distributed so that his center of gravity was proportional to his movement. The hand-polished blade was held low, pulled back next to his hip in the manner advocated by Rex Applegate. Out in front of him floated his left hand, its fingers twitching and jerking, the movement meant to distract his catlike opponent's eyes.

For his part, the merc adopted a bouncing type of approach. Weight forward on the balls of his feet, the Guatemalan darted forward, then leaped back, the machete's blade cutting a tight figure-eight pattern in the narrowing space between them. Their eyes were already locked in mortal combat, each hoping the other's concentration would be broken by the diversionary tactics they were hurling at each other. Neither of them were any longer aware of the clamor outside the house as the small church square began to fill with emergency-services personnel, reporters, and curious bystanders.

Silver moved first.

Rapidly shuffling forward, he closed the gap between them, feinting low toward the merc's belly. As the Guat countered by slashing downward and inside with his machete's blade, Jason hopped back, then struck with the knife's point. It caught the Latin killer just above the wrist as he attempted to recover from

Silver's ruse, opening a deep puncture that began oozing dark blood in a steady flow.

Stepping back and keeping his eyes on the now-grinning Ranger, the mercenary brought the dripping wound to his mouth and began sucking it. A broad smile creased his face, his eyes flickering with a strange inner light.

"Holy shit! You're a walking nightmare aren't you, boy?" Silver muttered loudly as he began to circle the figure.

Gripping the handle of his blade tighter, Jason grabbed an ashtray from an oval table still standing and threw it at the Latin's demonic face. As Crazy Horse instinctively ducked the flying object, the husky commando once again attacked, this time slipping inside the machete's sphere of influence to lock arms with the now-enraged Latino.

Spitting in each other's faces, Jason leaned back as the merc tried to bite his nose off. Butting hard with his forehead, Silver fought the nausea climbing up his throat as he drove the man's head back. Together they struggled, their muscles waging a war of endurance, knives gripped tightly as the deadly gambol began to reach a conclusion.

Jason recognized his opportunity. Darting forward, he sunk his teeth into a soft earlobe, jerking his head back with all the force he could muster. The ear stretched as far as the thick tissue would allow, then tore free. Crazy Horse screamed as the pain riveted him to a near standstill, an additional bolt of anguish exploding in his right foot as Silver drove his booted heel down, crushing the fragile bone structure like an eggshell.

Feeling the tide of the battle swing his way, Jason dropped his knife to the floor so that he could use both hands to twist the mercenary's machete free. Hearing it strike the hardwood surface, Silver grabbed a thick double handful of shirt, and dropping downward and back, flipped the hapless Latino head over heels.

Hooked together, the two performed a grotesque somersault across the floor, coming to rest just inside the ancillary doorway that Bannion had left open in his mad dash from the yard. Finding himself atop the dazed *mercenario*, Silver recognized the distinct shape of the frag grenade stashed inside a small bag hanging from the man's side. Balling up his fist, he struck the Latin twice in the nose, hearing the bone break and feeling the release of hot sticky blood as it splashed over him.

Jerking the lethal globe from its canvas prison, Jason pulled the pin holding the safety spoon in place. Beginning to count as he let it fly free, Silver scooted backward, shoving the grenade down the front of the moaning man's trousers as he reached a two-count. Quickly jerking the dazed merc to his feet, the diminutive night fighter swung the human time bomb around and pushed him through the open door. Stepping back, he braced himself against the room's inner wall just as the muffled explosion tore Crazy Horse in two.

It was then that he noticed the two feet sticking awkwardly out from underneath the shredded couch. Rushing over, he scooted the heavy piece of furniture off Bannion and hurriedly checked the agent's vitals. Patting him gently on the head, Silver breathed a sigh of relief. The big lug would be all right once he came to, although Jason doubted he'd appreciate the month-long headache he'd probably suffer as a result of the thumping he'd taken.

Realizing someone was banging on the front door with what sounded like the butt of a rifle, Silver picked himself up and headed for the entranceway. Outside, Bailey was in a lather, his guts aching as he wondered what he would find inside the papal retreat.

Melendez made a command decision. Cracking the library's door just enough to observe the hallway, he'd watched the two gringos spill from their rooms as his men began their attack on the house. For a moment he considered killing the tough-looking *cabron* who, only feet away from his hidden lair, collected Montalvo's bitch daughter. It was a fleeting thought, sobered by the realization that the other man would not hesitate to use the shotgun he held once he knew of Melendez's presence.

So instead of action, he waited, taking his time, setting the play up for the best possible results. He watched Thornton pass the silver automatic through the open door, then made note that both Maritza and the older gringo entered, locking the door behind them after the two North Americans exchanged words.

It was then that he'd stepped into the hallway, hoping to kill the outside man quickly, then attack those in the room. He knew the police were nearly upon them, and there hadn't been any gunfire from downstairs after the second grenade exploded. If his men were dead he needed to finish the Montalvos off and escape back the way he'd come.

Unfortunately the cold-eyed gringo spotted him before Melendez was set, snapping off a blast from the shotgun that nearly took his legs away. The major returned fire, sending a .44-caliber message down the hall, where the American was waiting for him to reappear. It, like the gringo's shot, missed.

Melendez believed in the old axiom that the best defense was a damn good offense. Leaping into the hall, he began loping down its length, the long-barreled Magnum held out front, thunderous explosions coming from its bottomless bore as the major squeezed off his remaining five rounds at Thornton's desperately moving figure.

If he could drive the man into another room, then use one of his three grenades to finish him, he would then only have to kick Montalvo's door in, throw his last two frags, wait out the detonations, and mop up with the shotgun.

But first, he needed to kill this bothersome gringo!

Time had run out for a good plan to come together. Thornton twisted violently to one side as Melendez materialized in the corridor, the massive Smith & Wesson 29 barking at him like a rabid dog. Dropping Wan's shotgun, Bo scrambled for his life, feeling chunks and splinters of wood striking all around him. Finding himself opposite the open door to his room, Thornton threw himself inside, rolling into the darkness like a gopher going for the gold.

Breathing hard from his unexpected sprint, Melendez dropped the empty revolver upon reaching the doorway Thornton had disappeared into. Swinging the riot gun around, he checked the chamber quickly, then altered his original plan. The gringo's own shotgun lay behind Melendez, left in the man's frenzied flight to escape death. The major remembered Thornton's loan of the pistol to whomever was behind the opposite door. That meant he was inside without a weapon.

I can use my shotgun to finish this bastard, thought Melendez. Then I'll take his and use it on the chickens in the next room.

Looking up, he heard the strangely muffled explosion of another grenade, satisfaction spreading across his coarse face as he realized at least one of the Guats was still in action. Taking a deep breath, the Butcher of El Refugio readied himself, then swung his beastlike frame into the doorway.

Thornton was waiting for him, the Russian springblade held tightly in both hands, his body prone in the middle of the floor. Seeing the major's figure enter the door, Thornton allowed his aiming instinct to go on automatic pilot. Depressing the firing lever, Bo felt the razor-edged blade fly free from the handle, a slight rasping sound escaping from the weapon as the spring released its several hundred pounds of pent-up energy.

The forged missile struck Melendez in the xiphoid, puncturing through the weakest part of the sternum, impaling the Latin's heart within a single massive beat. Eyes bulging in shock, the major staggered backward into the hall, jerking the shotgun's trigger out of reflex. The ensuing blast blew Thornton's window out, the downpour of shattering glass raining over Bailey, who stood directly under it.

Hearing the window break, the DEA man covered his head with his hands to protect himself. Silver, standing in the front door, watched in amusement as Calvin was drenched in glass. When the downpour was over, Jason, assuming his best English accent, spoke. "As you can see for yourself, *Mr.* Bailey, we haven't quite finished mopping up yet. . . ."

Peering out from under his armpit, Calvin glared at the straight-faced man whose clothing was stained with drying blood. "Outta my way, you son of a bitch!" he yelled, charging past Silver as though he'd been fired from a four-deuce mortar.

Looking out at the assembled throng in their front yard, Silver shrugged as if mystified by the whole episode, then quietly closed the door.

Upstairs Thornton climbed to his feet, his eyes on Melendez, who was bracing himself through sheer willpower against the wall opposite the doorway. Bo grimly watched the brutish assassin as he tugged at the embedded blade, slowly inching it out of his already-dead heart. Walking forward, Thornton stopped only a foot away from the hulking remains of Luis Melendez. Thornton's soul shivered as the major's coal black eyes focused on him, their depths empty, like that of an animal whose life is only a spark that operates the machine called body.

Melendez managed to pull the blade backward several inches. Capturing the dying man's eyes, Bo assumed a solid karate stance, pulling his right arm back so that his open palm was parallel to his chest. Smiling for just an instant, he twisted slightly as if winding up the muscles of his powerful body, then exploded with a forward thrust that slammed the lower portion of his callused palm into the springblade's aluminum stabilizer.

Melendez's spine arched mightily, raising the mass murderer up high on his toes as the knife bit savagely into what was left of his heart. Spewing bright arterial blood from his mouth, Major Luis Adolfo Garcia Melendez slid down the wall, dying at Thornton's feet while Bo watched passionless.

CHAPTER

16

Maritza Montalvo plopped herself into one of the deep leather chairs and watched Jason Silver methodically clean his Colt Commando. Although the carbine itself was broken down into what seemed like hundreds of pieces, Silver's Glock sat within hand's reach of the busy man, a twenty-round magazine stuffed into its grip. The girl could also see the black-handled combat thrower tucked snugly next to the small of his back, a momentary vision of the dead mercenary's severed head trampling across her memory like a frenzied horse. Maritza shuddered, hugging her sweater-clad shoulders as if it weren't a comfortable seventy-two degrees in the spacious den.

"Hey, Maritza." Silver's cheery voice snapped the girl back to the present. "How come you didn't want to attend the nosey news conference this morning? At least you would have gotten out of this place for a coupla hours."

The lithesome girl uncurled her long legs out from under a firm bottom, standing and stretching so that every feminine attribute silently announced its own erotic presence to the appreciative headhunter. If I ain't crying, I'm dying, Silver thought to himself. Fumbling the automatic sear in his thick hands, the former LRRP politely excused his roving eyes for their unabashed interest.

"The press only wants to ask a lot of silly questions of my father. 'Were you afraid?' 'Did anyone in the family get hurt?' 'Do you think the killers will try again?' They lack compassion, feelings. I have seen enough of that to last me a lifetime." Fin-

139

ished, she sauntered across the thickly carpeted floor to a wall lined with books, and began scanning the titles.

"Yeah, I hear you. Never did care much for the media. Most of the good ones end up dead or drunks, at least that's the way it seemed in the Nam."

Finding nothing to interest her, the girl walked around the table Silver was working at and leaned up against the far wall. Crossing her arms beneath her breasts, a calculated move causing them to bulge enticingly underneath the thin woolen sweater, she raised a question that had been nibbling at her since they'd hospitalized Mike Bannion two days earlier. "Mike is going to be okay, isn't he?"

Jason grunted. Damn SEALs, they always did seem to get the girls. "Oh sure," he replied. "The doc says he took a nasty thump on the noggin, and the gash needed twenty-five stitches to close. Not to mention all the bits of glass they pulled out of his fat ass, thanks to that damn grenade. . . . Other than that, he's just fine."

Maritza sighed. She was in love with the blond hunk whom Thornton credited with saving their lives. If he hadn't been alert and warned them when he did, the now-dead Major Melendez might have finished what he'd started at El Refugio. Hopefully, she thought, I'll have a chance to visit Mike. It's so *boring* sitting around this bombed-out prison!

"When will we be able to leave?" she asked.

Jason checked the Colt's firing pin again, finding a caked hint of carbon at its base and scraping it free with the point of his Swiss Army knife. Applying a light coat of oil with his fingers, he dropped the silver cap buster into the immaculate bolt, then plugged the cotter pin back into place. "The sergeant major heard from Bo this morning, before they took your parents to the media event. Looks like State's gonna let the papers and evening news play up Melendez's attack on you people, hopefully pulling the good *presidente*'s name into the fracas, then Lippman will announce State's awarding of political asylum tomorrow morning.

"That afternoon you'll jump on Air Force One and head for Washington, D.C., home of the ultimate puzzle palace, and throne of King George the First."

Biting her lip at the news, Maritza picked up a magazine and began leafing through it. Feigning attention to a picture of a group of nuns handing out food in Kentucky, she asked another question. "Jason, do you think I'll be able to visit Mike before we leave?"

Slipping the forward retention bolt through the weapon's upper receiver so that the rifle was once again in one piece, Silver looked up at the girl. "Dunno about that, babe. Up to Bo, although I wouldn't get your hopes up. We *think* we trashed everyone connected with hanging your heads out to dry . . . but that doesn't mean we can all go to the zoo and feed the monkeys."

"I understand," Maritza said. "I can always call Mike; Bo said he had a phone in his room. That, as my father says, would be the prudent thing to do."

Beginning to assemble his gutted magazines, Jason tossed a beaming smile at the lovely girl. "That's the ticket, Maritza. Mike would surely appreciate a call from you, and he'll understand why you can't come personally. After all, that's his job."

Making her mind up as she closed the periodical, dropping it back on the table's pile, Maritza assumed her most innocent face, the one that always worked on her father. "Are you hungry, Jason? I could fix you something from the kitchen."

"Food? Damn, it is nearly noon, isn't it? Yeah, I'd take one of them steak sandwiches you and your mom served up yesterday, if there's any meat left."

"Oh, I'm sure there is, Señor Silver. It'll take me only five minutes to prepare. Do you want chips, too?"

Jason pushed a bright cartridge onto the first magazine's guide plate, listening closely to the stiff spring as it compressed slightly under the minuscule weight of the round. "Chips? Sure. Maybe a glass of milk, too?"

"No hay un problema. It is no problem, Jason. I'll be back in two shakes of a goat's tail!" With that, the teenager headed for the kitchen, shutting the den door behind her as Silver forced himself not to turn and watch the girl's provocative bottom sashay past him.

Remembering he hadn't yet performed a function check on the Commando, Jason picked the weapon up, pulling the charging handle sharply to the rear. With a sinking feeling, he felt the bolt jam itself into the telescoping stock's aluminum tunnel, noticing at the same time he'd left the recoil spring assembly out when he'd slapped the rifle back together.

Speaking out loud although there was no one in the room to hear him, the man Bo Thornton considered to be his alter ego chided himself soundly. "Well, Jason, me boyo, what the hell do you expect? It's tough enough to put one of these plastic soul takers together when your head's on straight. No one said it was possible with a hard-on the size of Detroit snorting away in your pants. . . ."

Blushing, he opened the carbine and began tugging at the bolt's notched face. Maybe he could get the thing back together before the Latina fox returned with his lunch. By then, too, his aching manhood might have decided to stand down, allowing him to leave the table without embarrassing himself in front of the girl he was being paid to protect.

Azo's eyes flared as the Salvadoran watched Montalvo's daughter slip around the side of the damaged house. Why? he wondered. Following the girl's progress as she moved quickly to the still-unrepaired wrought-iron gate, he noted the way she kept looking back, as if she expected someone to be following her . . . or to catch her. With a wide grin of understanding, the answer came to Azo. She was *sneaking out*! For whatever reason, the girl was actually running away from her protectors. Azo believed in taking advantage of opportunity, no matter what prompted it. Watching the girl hurry across the plaza toward him, the Salvadoran merc knew he was being handed the solution to his problem.

Maritza didn't notice the priest until she nearly bowled him over. When she did, it was too late to avoid the man as he was smiling and asking her in Spanish whether or not she needed any help. He was dressed in the black garb of a man of God, although his face seemed somewhat cruel. Stopping, she performed the expected ritual of crossing herself before answering the priest's question, hoping Silver wouldn't come rushing from the house in search of her.

"May I help you, my daughter? You look worried, and in so much of a hurry for someone so young."

Attempting to meet the priest's gaze but failing under the intensity of his own, Maritza lowered her eyes, suddenly depressed because of her failure to see Bannion before they had to leave. "No, Father. I was only hoping to visit a friend. Thank you for your concern, I will return to my room now."

Stopping the somber girl as she turned, Azo slipped his arm under hers and asked where her friend was.

Sensing that perhaps she could charm this puzzling cleric into helping her, Maritza forced herself to face him, willing a child-like look of trust to cross her finely formed features. "He is in the hospital downtown, Father. He was badly hurt in the fight two days ago. I would like only to visit with him, to pray for his recovery. But now it seems that won't be possible."

The priest looked skyward as if thanking divine inspiration personally. Then he stroked her thick hair, his voice low, filled with concern. "A man who saves your life deserves prayer, especially if he has suffered because of the consequences of his actions. But you cannot go alone to the hospital, it would be unsafe.

"I believe Father Delgado would approve of my escorting you to see your friend. If you are comfortable with that, we can go in my car. It is parked out front, and I know the hospital of which you speak."

"Oh yes, Father. *¡Gracias!* I would enjoy your company very much." Stepping back from the priest's touch, Maritza gave him a bright smile, not knowing that it provoked the Salvadoran's lust for her even more than the fragrance of her perfume, and the obvious ripeness of her body.

"Good! We'll go right away. Do you need to tell someone anything before we leave?"

Casting a guilty eye toward the house, Maritza shook her head no. Then, together they began walking toward the street, the priest chatting nonstop about the virtue of visiting the sick, his right hand firmly closing above the girl's left elbow as he guided her from the safety of the church.

She knew something was wrong as soon as she shut the door behind her. The "priest" was already starting the car, a dark pair of sunglasses closing his eyes off to her. It was the car that was out of place, it was not the kind of automobile a Catholic priest would have available for his use. "I didn't know the church owned such fine vehicles," she said.

Azo, checking his rearview mirror for oncoming traffic, turned to the girl. "A beautiful woman should be escorted in style wherever she travels, *señorita*. Don't you agree?"

Before she could reply, Azo's hand snaked around the back of her neck, yanking her face first into his lap. Twisting her head so that she yipped in pain, the assassin pulled a Blackmoore Dirk from an ankle sheath hidden under his cassock, plunging the triangular point into a spot just below the terrified girl's right eye. A slow drop of blood pushed its way onto the polished steel, then began to creep down the length of the blade. Maritza stopped her struggling, a sad whimper escaping from her lips as she cursed her stupidity.

Azo spoke quickly, harshly, twisting the knife just enough to enforce his commands to the girl whose neck he held in an iron grip. "Fight me and I will blind you! All we want is for your father to meet with us, nothing more! Perhaps if we can talk, the problems between us can be solved with no further bloodshed. You would like that, no?"

The now-sobbing figure of the girl moaned, the sound one of utter defeat.

"Good, I knew you were a smart *chica*. I am going to take you to a place where we will call your father. It is comfortable, there is music, TV, things for you to do while we await his arrival.

"But . . . should you prove as foolish as you have already, my Wolves will hunt you down and bring you back to me.

"*If* they have to do that, Señorita Montalvo, I will be most unhappy, and *nothing* you can do afterward will please me. Do you understand?"

Maritza thought of Silver, now probably racing frantically through the house looking for her. He would hate her for her duplicity! She deserved whatever happened, for she was now the bait that would bring her father to his killers like a lamb offered up for sacrifice.

Gently tugging the knife free from its toehold, Azo turned her face upward so he was looking directly into the terror-stricken eyes. Speaking in Spanish, he told her how beautiful she was, how soft her hair felt in his hands, how much he wanted to spray himself inside her. Finished with his game, the hired killer pulled a set of police handcuffs from under the seat, snapping them around the shocked girl's wrists in two deft movements. Pulling her upright, he once again checked the sidewalk and street, satisfied that if anyone was watching, they hadn't the guts to intervene.

"We go now," he told her as the car inched forward into traffic. "Remember my promises to you, little one. Cry out, attempt to escape, anything at all, and you will feel Azo's knife as it slits your eyes out of your skull!"

Maritza sat as still as a pillar of salt. She no longer felt the puncture wound under her eye, no longer noticed the blood running down her cheek and onto her yellow sweater, no longer thought of Mike Bannion and how surprised he'd have been to see her next to his bed. She thought only of death, and how it stalked her every waking hour, making life a nightmare with ghouls like this bastard sitting next to her, whispering their filth into her ears.

She *would* try to escape as soon as there was a chance. Better she died in the attempt than to be the lure that brought her father to these butchers! Offering a silent prayer for strength as well as for forgiveness, Maritza tried to relax as the car turned onto a long street overlooking the sailboat-filled San Francisco Bay.

Jason Silver felt like a fool. When the girl hadn't returned in five minutes he should have gone looking for her, but he'd given her another five minutes because ... because he trusted her! *Damn stupid of you, Ranger! You should have paid more attention to all that shit about Bannion being in the hospital. As sure as hell serves hot dogs, she's on her way to see him, and that means she's a target for anyone still gunning for Ricardo's balls.* Silver paused at the front door, then turned and ran to the phone in the den. He would search the grounds *after* he called Bo. With a ten-minute head start, Maritza would be halfway to the hospital by now. Or, God forbid, halfway to the Libertadian embassy. Dialing Thornton's pager, he wished he were somewhere else. Bo would throw a bitch-fit upon hearing this news. He'd been suckered by the oldest trick in the book, and by a jeanful of swinging ass!

Hearing the triple beep at the pager's end, Jason asked Bo to call the hospital and ask for Maritza Montalvo, he then hung up, knowing Thornton would immediately understand his message. He then checked the Glock's chamber with a sharp tug of the slide to the rear, and began running.

CHAPTER

17

It was six o'clock that evening when Father Delgado received Azo's brief message. Hanging up the phone, the exiled priest closed his eyes and said a silent prayer for the girl whose muted screams were still echoing in his head. Animals! he thought. They are nothing but animals! Why God allowed such beasts to walk the face of his earth, Delgado could not fathom. Looking at those sitting in the tight office which was Delgado's only retreat from the outside world, he wondered how he would tell Ricardo Montalvo that he must give himself up in order for Maritza to have a chance at surviving her kidnappers' carnal brutalities.

Thornton, the only member of the team present, broke the oppressive silence following the call. Time was wasting away, he reminded himself. "So? What the fuck, Padre? What's this latest asshole want us to do?"

Delgado, waving a tired hand in front of him, answered. "Remember you are on holy ground, my son. Please control your language, especially in front of the *señora*.

"The man, and I use the term lightly, tells me that Maritza is alive. That is all. If we want to see the child again, Ricardo must meet the terrorists in four hours, I may accompany him.

"The *señora* is to remain here at the church; they only want Ricardo. If we follow their instructions, the girl will be turned over to me at the meeting place. If not . . ."

"If not, she'll be raped, tortured, and left in a garbage bag along I-Five for us to find three or four days from now," murmured Thornton to no one in particular. He'd heard this all before. The game never changed, only the players.

147

Mrs. Montalvo burst into tears, her husband wrapping his arm around her, staring hard at Thornton. "Your man failed us this afternoon, *señor*. If he'd been attentive this would not have happened!"

Bo stared the distraught man down. "May I remind you that it was *your* daughter who deceived Jason, who knew what she was doing and the danger it would put you all in. Silver feels bad enough about her disappearance, but I won't allow you to lay it all on his doorstep."

Delgado slammed his fist down, stunning everyone into silence. "We have no time for this. In less than four hours we must meet these devils, they say they only want to talk, to discuss a settlement with Ricardo. Aguilar wants peace now that the PPF has been recognized by the United Nations Assembly. With Ricardo at his side, he believes they can wage a political war against the insurgents which may turn the current tide."

"Holy shi—" Thornton, remembering the father's earlier admonition, corrected himself in midsentence. "Excuse me Father, but you of all people can't really *believe* that crap. From what I understand, you're not exactly Aguilar's favorite wafer passer. What makes you think they won't put a bullet in *both* your heads?"

Delgado nodded. "You are right, of course. But we have no alternative. They hold the girl. What else can we do?"

Montalvo spoke, his voice brittle. "Only what they have told us to do. I will meet the spawn of Melendez, and I would appreciate Father Delgado's company. They will not harm him, he is too popular, too influential. Not even Aguilar would be so foolish."

"I will accompany you, my son. God will watch over his children."

Thornton shook his head, unbelieving of what was happening in front of him. As much as he admired these two men, he couldn't help but question their common sense. He couldn't allow them to walk into the lions' den alone. "Well, we'll be there, too, just in case your guardian angels have their hands full elsewhere. Where's the meet to take place?"

The priest remained silent, his palms pressed together, eyes half-shut. Montalvo spoke, his own eyes on the bare wood floor of Delgado's study. "We will go alone, Mr. Thornton. You have done your job, and I imagine you have been paid well. This is something I must do if Maritza is to live and return to her mother.

"Besides, how can I trust you?"

Thornton started in his chair, eyes afire at the question. "What the fuck kind of bullshit is that, Ricardo? We've risked our collective asses for you people ever since springing you from the hotel. The little jubilee that put Mike in the hospital wasn't exactly touch-fucking-football. . . . What do you mean, 'How can I trust you?'"

Montalvo left his chair and walked to where Thornton was seated. As at the conclusion of their lunch, he placed his small hands upon the big commando's shoulders, and with a sad grin, whispered so that only the two of them could hear. "When you came to our bedroom the other night, you knew it was Melendez who was outside. You *knew* this, Bo. How could you know such a thing if you hadn't been warned before?

"I didn't think about it then, only yesterday when my mind was more tranquil. You said nothing to me about that bastard being alive, not to mention being here in San Francisco. You betrayed my trust, *amigo*. That is why I cannot allow you to jeopardize tonight's meeting."

Thornton was shaken. Damn them! he roared internally. Damn Lippman and all the other scum that pulled their strings like puppets!

Montalvo continued, seeing the anguish in his friend's pleading eyes. "You had your orders, Bo. I now have mine. It was a good race, no? But now there is no other way."

Turning to his wife, the man whom Thornton had grown to admire and trust motioned the graceful woman to join him. "Father Delgado? I will meet you here in three hours, then we will go. I wish now to be left alone with my wife. We have things to talk about."

Delgado nodded his agreement, standing and indicating with his eyes that he expected Thornton to leave with him. When they were out the door, the priest turned and spoke, his eyes misty looking in the frail light of the dim hall. "Forgive us, *señor*. We have fought the beast for many years now, and to have it end this way after coming so close is crushing. Ricardo will do as he must, and I will bring the girl back to her mother. It is God's will."

Watching Delgado's back as he departed to prepare himself at the altar, Thornton couldn't help but wonder who in the last ten minutes had asked God what the heck his will was? Seems somebody's making decisions for you, sir, mused the freedom fighter. Perhaps Saint Peter needs more than a prayer and a few Hail Marys this time around, maybe that old warrior needs a few good men to kick a little ass. Maybe Father Delgado dialed the wrong damned phone number when he was clacking his beads together. In any case, *this* old boy ain't gonna sit around and let Montalvo meet his maker without the proper introduction!

Striding down the hallway, Thornton reminded himself of the motto he'd lived his professional life by, the Latin words burned into his subconscious so deeply he'd never be able to root them out.

De oppresso liber—to free them from oppression.

Damn right!

CHAPTER

18

"What the hell do you mean, we're to pull off Montalvo? On whose orders? What kind of diplomatic weirdness are you laying on me now, Cal!" Thornton's knuckles were white as he attempted to crush the hard plastic receiver in his hand. Behind him, the team was waiting, listening intently to the one-sided conversation Bo was having with their DEA contact, Calvin Bailey.

"Screw Lippman!" Bo shouted. "Montalvo's walking into an ambush, we both know that. This goofy priest isn't going to do diddly-squat except get his own ass greased, and Maritza is probably dead already. What's State's big problem with letting us finish the job they hired us for?"

Thornton listened for the next few minutes while the frustrated agent at the other end repeated what he had been told by one Richard Lippman.

The news wasn't good.

"Bo," pleaded Bailey, "State went directly to Aguilar via our ambassador to La Libertad as soon as the abduction was reported. The colonel denies any knowledge of the hit by Melendez, claims he'd only just learned the major was tied into the PPF. . ."

Thornton gagged inwardly. "That's bullshit, Calvin! Melendez was public enemy number one to the PPF. They're probably dancing in the streets right now, and we're probably considered minor saints down there. . . . 'Tied to the PPF' my big ass!"

Bailey, sitting in the tiny office afforded him by the local DEA station chief, grabbed another cigarette from the near-empty pack. "Yeah, I know it stinks. Aguilar says he sent a team of 'police officials' to bring Melendez back. They're probably the same guys who grabbed the girl. Our ambassador feels Montalvo will get a decent trial *if* he can be recovered and sent back to La Libertad.

"State is of the opinion the whole ball game is out of control at this point. The media is going nuts looking for spooks and gooks, Aguilar is promising reforms at home and claiming Montalvo rigged this whole kidnap to embarrass him. The PPF is raising hell at the U.N., saying the colonel planned the attack on Montalvo to look like a PPF terrorist action. . . . It's crazy, just plain nuts."

Thornton could hear the distraction in his friend's voice. Poor Cal, he thought. He's getting blasted by everyone to include me, and he hasn't done anything but his damn job! "Okay, listen up, squid. I'm going after Ricardo tonight. But I need to know where they're meeting these assholes, and when. I *know* you sneaky devils have tapped every phone this monument to the Pope has, so how about giving me the poop I need to bury these clowns?"

A long smoggy silence followed. Bo began drumming his fingers on the desk top, aware of Silver's and Frank's mute silence behind him. Finally, Calvin spoke. "I can't do that, Bo. Lippman already called the secretary. Springblade is to terminate the mission as of right now. It's out of my hands."

Thornton exploded. Behind him, Silver rolled off the couch, staring in awe at the man's raw energy as he yelled into the phone. Hartung merely sat back in his chair with a huge sergeant major's smile on his craggy face. He knew NCO talk when he heard it. "Now you listen to me, maggot! Our deal says once this team hits the field, *no-fucking-body* can pull us off until the bodies are cold. Ronnie-baby agreed to that little caveat, and as far as I know, King George knows the rules, too.

"So I don't give a fat rat's ass about Lippman, State, or His Lowness the Secretary. No wonder that kraut wouldn't take a lie-detector test! With all the bullshit he's slung, he'd burn the damned machine out once they got past his friggin' name.

"I gave Montalvo my *word*, Cal. My *word*! He already knows that we set him up for the Melendez deal. . . ."

"How?" asked Bailey.

"'Cause he's one of those rare people who listens when you talk to him, that's how. I slipped up when the hit was coming down, mentioned the scumbag's name out of school, he remembered afterward."

"And now he thinks you're lower than whale shit, right?"

Thornton sighed. "Roger that. That's why I gotta go after him tonight. I won't be able to live with this if he buys the rancho. Please, Cal. You got the power, give it to me!"

Calvin Bailey flipped the still-burning cigarette into the trash can next to his borrowed desk. Probably cause a damned three-alarm fire, he thought without remorse. Making his decision, he pushed the door closed with his foot. Disregarding the fact his own phone was probably tapped, he gave the big man what he needed. "The zoo, reptile exhibit, twenty-two hundred hours. I'll meet you."

"Negative!" barked Thornton. "We'll go it alone. You call Billings and tell him we're going to terminate the mission, all right, *after* we terminate the terminators. Have him jump through his ass and get to the president. The secretary can hang this one in his ear, we're taking Aguilar down tonight!"

"Good luck, pal," Bailey said, then was gone.

Hanging up, Thornton took a moment to compose himself. He'd assumed the other two men would go with him, but he hadn't asked them formally. If the sanction was indeed off, they could end up in a world of hurt by backing him up. They had a right to know, to make up their own minds. He'd understand no matter which way they chose to go.

Turning, his chest swelled with pride as he watched both men picking up their weapons and preparing to leave. Hartung, a crusty tone to his already-gruff voice, nodded in Bo's direction. "You ready, Jason?" he asked.

The ex-LRRP zipped up his jacket, pulled a black watch cap over his head, then jacked a round into his Colt's chamber. "Does the Pope shit in the woods? Is a bear Catholic? Damn right, I'm ready!"

"Then let's do it." Both men looked at Thornton, who was now standing, Wan's shotgun cradled in his massive arms.

"Airborne and amen," replied Frank.

"Eat shit and die," added Silver. "I got a score to settle with an asshole I haven't even met yet!"

Outside, the moon grabbed a dark cloud, hiding its full face from the horror it knew was coming.

CHAPTER
19

The San Francisco Zoo is one of the largest exhibitions of exotic animals in the world. Visitors flock to its gates on a year-round basis, eager to spend the day wandering beautifully landscaped grounds, their Nikon, Pentax, and Olympus cameras capturing staged photographs to be pressed into thick family albums as reminders of this magnificently choreographed urban jungle.

At night after closing, workers fan out to clean, feed, and water the scores of creatures which populate this artificial animal kingdom. One of the most celebrated displays is the reptile exhibit, where literally hundreds of snakes, lizards, amphibians, and other dragonlike monsters are confined in glass or concrete holding areas for their observers' visual enjoyment. The most impressive of these is the Alligator Pit, a huge cement mock-up of tropical flora and fauna where a wide selection of both alligators and crocodiles can be found sunning themselves under high-intensity lamps.

The alligator itself is a member of the *crocodilus* family. He differs from the crocodile in that his snout is shorter and broader, and when closing his lower jaw, hundreds of surgical-edge teeth slam themselves into specially designed pits instead of marginal notches as found in his cousin's maw. Both members of the species are unable to actually chew their food. Instead, they survive by dragging their prey underneath the water and drowning it. Afterward, the beast will stuff the unfortunate victim beneath a sandbar, or between a tangle of underwater roots until the remains soften enough for the animal to begin tearing off and gulping down huge portions of rotting meat.

155

Although highly regarded as suitcase material, alligators make poor pets, as evidenced by anyone in New·York City who has been forced to flush one down the toilet when it outgrew their mysteriously vanished kitten's sandbox. Overall, alligators and their thuglike relatives are ugly, brutish, and slow-witted... reminding many of the more astute visitors of certain politicians and their wives.

It was amid these foul creatures that Azo chose to meet with Montalvo and the priest. Instructing his two henchmen to pull a quick reconnaissance of the building while he waited with the unconscious girl, the Salvadoran soldier-for-hire mused as to which of the two men he would kill first. Both were equally acceptable candidates, although the priest was certainly a more entertaining prospect.

Noting the double blip of a hand-held penlight, Azo checked Maritza's bonds. She was heavily sedated and lying in the sedan's backseat, a space blanket arranged so that it covered her from head to toe. Besides the knife prick, Azo hadn't harmed the girl, knowing he might need her as a bargaining chip should things fall apart at the last moment. He believed in always considering the worst-case scenario, or what his gringo instructors called "Murphy's Law." It hadn't taken much to convince one of the embassy's secretaries, a Libertadian woman known in certain diplomatic circles for her ability to suck the chrome off a bayonet, to rant and rave in the background as Azo discussed an exchange with Delgado. He relished the effect their little ruse must have had on the holier-than-thou clergyman, especially with the girl's parents in the same room.

Before exiting the vehicle, he checked the magazine of his Ruger Government .22-caliber automatic, giving its flat black suppressor a final twist so that it was fastened securely to the pistol's long barrel. Patting his Banana Republic safari jacket's large cargo pocket, the hit man assured himself that he was carrying an additional three magazines of .22 Hornet ammunition. Slipping the perfectly balanced handgun into a snug leather shoulder holster, Azo then pulled the Blackjack Mamba combat knife from its nylon scabbard. Nine full inches of rolled-edge steel became an extension of his hand, the blackened blade reflecting only the killer's immediate intentions. With luck he'd be able to add three new bones to his already-impressive collection.

Stepping from the car, he made sure all four doors were locked before heading toward the darkened building. It was just 2130 hours, according to his military watch, so they had a half hour before Montalvo was to show. Meeting the two Wolves, Azo instructed the one known as Alfonso to act as their outside security. He'd have only the main entrance to watch as all other exits were locked for the evening. When their quarry arrived, "Alf," as he was affectionately known to his *amigos*, would allow them to enter the exhibit.

Taking the second assassin with him, Azo quickly picked the door's simple lock and slipped inside the climate-controlled hall. Dim lights guided the two human reptiles as they made their way to the Pit. All around them, they heard the slithering of snakes against thick-paned glass, the crack of tiny teeth snapping together, and the rustle of clawed toes scampering across sandy terrain models.

For some reason Azo felt his dick getting hard. Perhaps it's the atmosphere he thought, dark images of having Montalvo's daughter on the highly polished floor while his men and the scaly creatures surrounding them watched, surfaced like a hand from the grave.

Dismissing his momentary lapse in concentration, the Salvadoran quickly found the Alligator Pit through a maze of passageway which led to it from several different directions.

The room itself was a cavernlike affair with a high domed ceiling and skylights which allowed natural sunshine or starlight to enter. A broad walkway surrounded the Pit, chain-link fencing preventing curious tourists from accidently feeding the animals with their sometimes clumsy children. A wide pool of circulating water was home to over fifty of the beasts. A man-made sandbar sat like a lily pad in its center, allowing room for ten to fifteen alligators to bask themselves under artificial lighting. A perimeter of carefully constructed jungle habitat completed the facade, its nooks and crannies home for the rest of the huge lizards.

The most unique feature of the display was a narrow bridge which traversed the pool from end to end. By using it, visitors could stare down into the moat itself, watching with wide eyes as the reptiles frolicked just feet below them. A wide safety net constructed of wire mesh was strung below and to the sides of the bridgeway, just in case someone slipped or leaned too far out over the handrail. Hidden in a small niche on the south wall was a hand crank which allowed for the netting to be rolled back for repair or replacement.

Standing on the walkway, Azo directed the second Wolf to reel back the safety lattice. Watching as it slowly retreated in either direction, he smiled at the bright golden orbs staring up at him from the pit's depth. "Soon, my children," he whispered to them. "Soon you will have a great feast. I promise you."

The hollow sound of hard-soled shoes slapping against tiled flooring echoed down one of the hallways. "Azo, they come!" murmured his accomplice.

"*¡Si, encontramos aquí!* We will meet them here, on the bridge. I will kill the padre first, as he feels immortal because of his standing in the press. It is he who may give us the hardest time, believing us afraid of harming him.

"Montalvo will be next. After I have finished them off, come to me from your position against the wall, and together we'll dump them into the pool. That should make our scaly friends happy, sick as they probably are of fish guts and raw pork!"

Both executioners laughed, the echo swallowed up by the exhibit's cultivated environment.

"They got here about five minutes ago," whispered Silver. Thornton grunted in acknowledgment. Several paces away, Hartung knelt next to the car they'd just removed Maritza's slumbering form from. Taking it to their own vehicle, a custom van with all the amenities of home, the sergeant major laid her on the bed and covered her snugly with a wool blanket.

"Just doped up, that's all. Coupla cuts, a bruise maybe. She'll be fine."

"Think she was raped, Frank?"

"Nope. I took the liberty of checking her underclothes, everything's in place and in one piece. They're saving her for something, maybe a hostage, I don't know. In any event they didn't want to damage the goods before taking Ricardo out."

The two men finished their leader's recon, easily locating the Wolf at the entrance to the exhibit hall. Working their way back to Jason, they were now planning their next move.

"Just Delgado and Montalvo show up?" asked Thornton.

"Roger that, boss. They parked somewhere further down the parkway, then walked up the street. Somebody met them at the doors, patted them down, then sent them inside."

Hartung, ensuring his Browning's magazine was in place, spoke. "Yeah, we saw the dirtball while we were creepy-crawling around the objective. He's kinda careless, didn't seem to have a rifle or anything on him. You can figure on a handgun, though."

Bo looked at Silver in the faint glow of the streetlights lining the broad walkways. "You think you're good enough to take that bastard out?"

Jason grinned, his face looking almost demonic. "Shit, Sarge," he spat, "give me a minute or two and he'll be food for the worms."

"Do it," replied Thornton, touching the man in encouragement. "We'll wait 'til you signal, then Frank and I are going in. Watch the front in case more company arrives. The girl's in the van, you've got the keys."

Silver nodded once, then eased his way into the darkness.

Padding silently along a well-worn groundkeeper's path, Jason made his way to within twelve feet of the guard before coming to a halt. The man was standing sideways to him, the blunt shape of a heavy-frame revolver hanging from his hand. The ground around him was open, offering no further cover for Silver to make his approach on.

"Looks like you and me, sweetheart." Fishing beneath his dark cotton pullover, the hard-core Springblader slipped a McEvoy 4 from one of the two sheaths he was carrying. The knife flew flatter than the Viper at short distances like the one facing him.

Raising himself to his feet, Silver adopted a classic throwing stance. Placing his left foot forward and drawing back his right arm, Jason chose to deliver the fourteen-ounce piece of sharpened steel using the handle grip. Hours of practice had taught him that at the distance he was now from his target, the blade would make one complete turn in the air before striking. Exhaling slowly, he clicked his tongue loud enough for the man to turn in his direction, offering the blades man an unobstructed view of his chest.

Silver's arm exploded forward, the knife leaving it as if it were on fire. Whistling through the cool night air, it struck Alf at the base of his throat, cleaving inward, splitting his larynx so that no sound escaped his twisted lips. Even as the man sank downward, both hands fruitlessly tugging at the knife's slabbed handle, Jason moved in for the kill.

Reaching the dying man in three huge bounds, Silver delivered a snap kick to the Wolf's belly. Still not satisfied, the night warrior stepped back and fired another one into the helpless figure's right temple. An audible pop told him he'd crushed the fragile bone structure, the impact powerful enough to kill by itself.

Waiting an extra second, Silver fought to control his breathing as nature's own speed continued to inject itself into his system. Using his foot, the Viper firmly gripped in one hand, Jason rolled the dead man over. "It was all personal, asshole!" he muttered, picking up the penlight that had fallen from the guard's breast pocket and flashing it twice toward where Thornton and Frank were waiting.

In seconds, both men were at his side, staring down at the crumpled mass of dark clothing. Silver, wiping the throwing knife's blade clean in the close-cropped grass, looked up at Thornton. "You guys better get going. I'll let you know if any more munchkins like this puke show up."

"Nice work, Jason. We didn't hear a thing except you kicking the shit outta him."

Silver's teeth shone in the light coming from inside the building. "Thanks, Sergeant Major. Makes up for me losing the girl in the first place."

"Wasn't your fault," said Thornton. "She could have slipped one past any of us; you just happened to be there."

"Thanks, Bo. But it was still my fuckup."

"We'd better haul ass," urged Hartung. "You two can kiss and make up after we've pulled Ricardo and the priest's nuts outta the fire!"

In an instant both men were up the steps and inside, their

passing causing no more disturbance than the breeze they left in their wake.

Azo pointed the silenced Ruger at a spot between Montalvo's eyes, watching the man's reaction as he accepted death. The priest stood silently by, a step behind the doomed man but closer to the low guardrail on the walkway over the pit. The gunman had not bothered to introduce himself, feeling it was both foolish and pointless. Who wanted to know the name of the man who killed him? That kind of *mierda* only happened on *Miami Vice*, one of Azo's favorite television sitcoms.

"I am praying for your soul, *señor*." It was the priest, his hands folded piously in front of him as he silently mouthed words to a god Azo no longer believed in. "This is a terrible thing you do, my son. Be done with it and give me the girl! We have kept our part of your murderous bargain!"

The Salvadoran began to take up what little slack the pistol's trigger possessed. Just before the firing pin fell to strike the tiny round's brass rim, Azo smoothly swung the gun so that its long barrel lined up on Delgado's shiny forehead. "*¡Chinga su madre, tu hijo de una puta!*" he blurted as the souped-up .22 split the hard, bony surface of Father Delgado's skull, driving unmercifully forward, mushrooming deep inside the celebrated priest's brain.

Even as the black-robed corpse somersaulted over the narrow railing to land atop three massive reptilian bodies, Azo's death dealer was tracking back on target, Montalvo stunned into submission at the casual killing of his friend and confidant.

"Okay, now that we've dispensed grace to the good father, we can conclude our deal without further homilies or—"

The metal-to-metal slapping sound of a silenced weapon cut the Salvadoran's words off as Hartung belted two subsonic tongue twisters into the second guard, whose attentions had been focused too long on his leader's performance. A split second later, Thornton's 645 spit fire as he tried to zero the killer from the cover of the wide doorway both men were kneeling in. Combat reactions taking over, Azo's gun hand was already swinging toward the two intruders when one of Bo's .45 caliber gut busters struck it squarely in the upper receiver group. The force of the impact tore the small-caliber weapon from the Salvadoran's grip flinging it downward, where it landed in the now-frenzied waters of the pit.

Montalvo attempted to spin around, hoping to create some distance between himself and the priest's killer so that Thornton could finish the bastard off without fear of hitting his friend. The ballsy Latino hadn't taken two steps before he felt an arm like leather cord wrap around his throat, pulling him backward and in front of the now-screaming trigger man's body. Thinking to break free, Montalvo froze as the unholy sharp edge of Azo's midnight black Mamba cut him from the lobe of his ear to the base of this throat.

"Drop your weapons!" yelled the Salvadoran. "If you don't obey me, I will cut his head off and feed him to my hungry friends!"

Hartung, his Browning's front sight squarely locked on Azo's sweating face, looked to Thornton. The Special Operations veteran shook his head slowly, lowering his own handgun at the same time. "It's too long a shot, Frank. Too much of a chance of hitting Ricardo; let's hold for a minute and see what this jerk wants."

"You're calling it, Bo," replied the sergeant major, a bitter lump growing in his throat. "But I'd sure like to try, just for the fuck of it!"

Azo adjusted Montalvo so that he now stood directly between the two invaders, blocking any snap shot they might have been stupid enough to take. Drawing the reversed-curve blade along his captive's throat so that a thin sliver of bright red blood began to cascade down the taut brown skin, the Salvadoran barked a command for both men to throw their pistols into the pit. As they complied without speaking, Azo relaxed somewhat. Now it was time to get out of here, taking this political pig with him as insurance until he could reach the car. Then he'd open Ricardo Montalvo up like a can of beans, right in front of his beautiful daughter, who with any luck would be awake enough to witness her father's wide-eyed transition from life to death.

"Step forward!" he commanded. "I want to see your faces!"

Thornton indicated Frank should go first, blocking the big ~~ndo~~'s frame long enough for him to slip the Russian knife ~~om~~ its sheath.

When both men were directly under the dome's low glare lights, Azo studied them. One he did not know, that was certain. But the other? He was familiar, very familiar. "You! Old man! You leave, *now*!"

"Who's this flaming asshole calling an 'old man'?" growled Frank.

"Gotta be you, Frank. I don't remember Moses the way you do."

"Fuck you, Thornton. Just do me a favor and cut this cum bubble's balls off before you feed his nasty ass to the critters, okay?"

"You got it, brother. Tell Silver to call for an ambulance, and get Bailey down here ASAP."

"Airborne and—"

"Amen. Now move your ass, troop. I don't want any witnesses to what I'm gonna do to this cherry motherfucker!"

After Hartung departed, Azo ordered Thornton onto the bridge, wanting a closer look at the man's face. When Bo was several arm's lengths away, his memory clicked, bringing a smile to the merc's lean face. "*Now* I remember you! You and your team trained my company several years ago. I was just a lance corporal then, a machine gunner who wanted to become a *recombate*! You trained me well, Master Sergeant Thornton. Do you remember?"

"Fuck no, Julio. Why were you so special that I'd remember your dumb ass?"

Spitting his words past Montalvo's scabbing ear, the former recon specialist answered Thornton's deliberate prodding. "You remember Conchauga, my Sergeant?"

Thornton answered in Spanish, remembering the village where a single indig recon team held off two companies of the FMLN's best in an all-night siege. Calling in gunships and jet aircraft on their own position, the team had taken ninety percent casualties. Only two of the original five lived. This evil bastard was one of those survivors. "Yes. You and your friend fought well. I remember when we flew in to extract you and the dead. It was a valiant stand."

Azo's eyes clouded over at the memory. "Yes, a 'valiant' fight. Enrique was killed in ambush soon after you left. I fought for six, maybe seven more months. Then I left El Salvador, finding a better job with *mi* Colonel Aguilar in La Libertad!"

"So now you butcher old men and young women? Really stepped up in the world, didn't you?"

"I fight for myself these days!" roared Azo. "Not for false promises, gringo ideals, or weak politicians. All I know how to do is fight! That's all you gringos have taught us, it's all we'll ever be. . . ."

Montalvo, feeling the Mamba's edge lift from its perch at his throat, raised a heavy shoe and smashed it hard into his captor's upper foot. As Azo screamed in rage at the sudden jolt of pain, Thornton whipped his left hand out and grabbed Ricardo's shirt front. Pulling him away from the Salvadoran, Bo flung the frightened man behind him, bringing the unsheathed springblade into view. "Run!" he ordered. "Maritza's outside with the others, she's okay!"

Watching the enraged merc closely, Bo listened as Montalvo's footsteps dropped away in the vastness of the dome. "You and me, pal," he said in a low voice.

Azo, stepping back and fighting the dull throb of his injured foot, glanced over into the pit. All that was left of the priest was a shred of cloth from his cassock and a growing crimson stain in the dirty water that now hid his body. Returning his attention to Thornton, the murderous merc deftly spun the Mamba as if it were a living thing.

"Very pretty," cooed Thornton, gripping his own knife securely as he dropped into a modified Weaver stance. "Didn't catch your name in all the fuss, sure would like to know it before one of us dies."

Forgetting his own rule, the Salvadoran answered the crouching figure before him, knowing as he did so he'd lost the necessary edge between them. "Aguilar calls me Azo," he said quietly.

Thornton nodded. "Fitting. 'The Knife's Wound.' Very appropriate of the good colonel."

As the Salvadoran sprang forward, Thornton released the ⸮ ⸮d blade from its aluminum housing. Spinning sideways to ⸮ ⸮e merc's headlong rush, he watched the double-edged projectile catch Azo in midstride, burying itself to the hilt in the assassin's upper gut.

Hearing the Mamba strike the wooden planks of the walkway, Bo stepped in to grab the fatally wounded man from behind. Shoving him hard against the railing, Thornton leaned forward and whispered harshly into the mercenary's ear. "Azo, you dishonor the memory of Enrique and all the other brave sons of bitches who are still humping a ruck out there! Aguilar may call you Azo, but the man who's killed you thinks 'Asshole' is a more fitting title!"

With that, the powerful night stalker lifted the futilely struggling figure above his head, and with a mammoth thrust threw him far out into the gator-filled waters of the pit.

Hartung was the first to meet him as Bo walked out of the exhibit. All around them, emergency lights were flashing, the scene an all-too-familiar one to Thornton. Greeting Frank with a slight nod, Bo walked quickly to where Montalvo was holding his daughter in a rib-crushing embrace.

"You kill that kid in there?" asked Frank before they reached the sobbing father and child.

"Roger that, Frank. He joined that poor bastard Delgado, but I've a feeling that the priest went on to a higher calling than our friend Azo."

Bailey appeared out of nowhere, grabbing Thornton and urging him into the van. "Sergeant Major!" he barked. "Get the team in here ASAP! The fucking TV people are on their way and I want us to *di-di* most *rik-tic*."

"You got it, squid," replied the man who was old enough to be Bailey's long-lost daddy. "Just see if you can find an all-night liquor store on the way. I believe we all deserve a bottle or two of Jack Daniels for this one!"

"Airborne and amen!" concurred Silver, struggling to control the hot flush that was rising along his neck from the intensity of Maritza's thankful kisses after her rescue.

"Silver," jokingly warned a grinning Frank Hartung, "you use my line one more time and I'll kick your skinny ass from here back to Oregon!"

Behind them a gaggle of reporters were churning around the Montalvos as Lippman arrived on the scene, a Capitol Hill smile on his face and a prepared statement in his hand.

Ricardo Montalvo and family were now officially guests of the United States government.

CHAPTER

■■■■■■

20

La Libertad—Sources in the capital city of San Volcan confirmed that the president of this small country fled during the night in a military aircraft. Reports are conflicting, but accounts coming from members of Aguilar's staff indicate that millions of American dollars were looted from the country's Banco Nacional prior to the dictator departing.

The Swiss ambassador to La Libertad issued a communiqué early this morning stating his belief that President Aguilar may be seeking asylum in the Republic of Panama, where he enjoys cordial relations with that country's strongman, General Manuel Noriega.

Aguilar's rapid departure from the country is said to be directly connected to last week's murder of an exiled Catholic priest whose Sanctuary Movement was responsible for the safety of Ricardo Montalvo and his family while the U.S. State Department investigated charges of murder against the popular Socialist political leader.

Montalvo, rumored to be en route to the capital on a United States Air Force jet, was snatched from the jaws of death in a bizarre shoot-out at the San Francisco Zoo. Richard Lippman, the new U.S. ambassador to La Libertad, attributes quick thinking on the part of the FBI Special Rescue Team, which interdicted Aguilar's second group of assassins just as they were ready to kill Montalvo and his daughter.

> In that shoot-out, all three members of the
> death squad were killed, to include a Salva-
> doran mercenary linked with several major po-
> litical assassinations over the last year. No FBI
> agents were injured.

Linda rolled over on her back, holding the newspaper so that it
shielded her eyes from the balmy sun baking them both on
Thornton's deck. Bo had returned several days ago, phoning
ahead and asking her to prepare a few days' things so they could
stay up on his property. She'd happily done so.

Glancing over at him, the tawny brunette told herself that this
mission had been far different than the first one he'd taken. When
he'd returned from the carnage of Alpine, Thornton's mood was
sullen, almost fatalistic. This time he seemed released from some
invisible bond, his attitude positive as he worked around the
property and finished loose ends on the deck.

He hadn't even scolded her about the cracked spoiler on the
Corvette.

Now he sat several feet away from her, nude, a pair of Blue-
Blocker sunglasses shading his eyes. "What are you reading,
Bo?" she asked.

Holding up the magazine so she could see its cover, the vixen
who shared Thornton's life these days shook her head. "What the
hell is *Fighting Knives* about? Or do I want to know?"

Thornton chortled, adjusting himself so that he could better
watch the crashing surf pounding the snow white beaches far
below them. "It's a magazine about all those things nice liberals
like yourself pretend don't exist. Which makes it my kind of
reading!"

Arching her smooth back, Linda crawled over next to the man
she now was sure she loved. Pouring a thick pool of tanning
lotion into her palm, she began to slowly rub it along the fronts of
his legs, then up onto his belly. "Uh-oh! Who do we have here?"
she asked as Thornton's temperature began to rise.

"That's my 'liberal-buster,'" Bo growled back, "and he's
homing in on one right now!"

Rolling over on the laughing girl, Thornton smoothed her

thick hair back, kissing her lightly on the forehead. "Miss me?" he asked.

"Kinda."

"What should we do with all that money I brought home?"

Rubbing his back with her hands, Linda pursed her full lips a moment. "I think you have enough to start seriously looking for furniture . . . with my help naturally."

Thornton bent his head so that he could kiss the girl deeply. Coming up for air, he couldn't help but pose a question to her, knowing full well what the response would be. "You want to do that now or later?"

Linda pinched him hard on the ass, then began caressing him frantically. "Later," she whispered as the sun became a thousand times brighter. "Much, much later."